Cyanide

Emily Hagenbaugh

Published by Emily Hagenbaugh, 2022.

CYANIDE

First edition. January 26, 2022.

ISBN: 978-6-27-750567-7

Written by Emily Hagenbaugh.

Dedicated to Elizabeth Brown, Louise Macklin, and Danalynn Donovan!

Thanks ladies for your hard work to help make this novel the best it can be! I'm forever grateful!

Also dedicated to my family for all their love and support! I love you all so much!

Pilot

A crashing sound could be heard as waves ate at the sand. Stars lit up the night sky with their twinkling, showing the world their pictures. The light of the moon glistened on the water. With the sound of crashing, a gentle rustling came from the palms as they swayed, a hammock rocked along in rhythm. To a person walking by, they could spot a home within the dark.

POP POP POP!

Loud gunshots broke the silence, followed by a haunted howling.

As quick as the noise came, silence filled the home and a strong metallic stench reached the occupants' noses. A man stood above a dying woman, his eyes dulled with regret. The gun steady in his hands still aimed at the woman who was lying in a deep red puddle. His body was strong and sturdy, but his mind raced in sync with his heart.

"Finally. I didn't want it to come to this, but I couldn't let you poison him," the man said. "I would've come sooner, but you really pulled a Carmen Sandiego on me."

Her body trembled as she stood on unsteady legs, the tremors grew when she giggled. Underneath her breath, she muttered words in what sounded like Latin and a skeletal wolf's paw replaced her own arm. She stabbed the man in the stomach and yanked her blood soaked claw violently out, and watched with satisfaction as the man slid to the floor, clutching his wound.

"Ironic, isn't it? They ordered you to kill me, and they ordered me to kill you. Like something out of a movie. It's tragic, but I can't bring myself to care," she said.

The man sneered at the woman and took a painful breath in, aggravating his wounds.

"Very ironic, but as I said, sweetheart, I didn't want this," he said.

"Then why? I quit The Syndicate. You should've quit The Organization. Hell, I took a bigger risk coming back here," the woman shot back.

The man coughed, then spat out a glob blood and cleared his throat painfully. "I couldn't let you poison him."

"Poison...that's a laugh...I co-could say t-the same a-about you," she said weakly.

With a scoff, she fell to the floor. The last of her strength was gone. Both man and woman laid there on the kitchen floor, bleeding out. The two prayed that their six-year-old, who was still sleeping, had heard nothing. Their hearts dropped when they heard the pitter-patter of little feet.

"Mommy? Daddy? Are you okay? Why is the floor all red? Did you spill ketchup everywhere?" the six-year-old asked.

The dying parents wanted to comfort and reassure their little boy, but they couldn't. Neither of them could move as they spent their energy, and they lost more blood.

"Mommy? What's wrong? Do you need the doctor?" the little boy asked.

Not receiving an answer, the little boy raced out of the room and dialed 911. By the time the ambulance got there, both parents had passed, leaving a sobbing and heartbroken six-year-old behind.

11 Years Later

Seventeen-year-old Fox Kane walked the halls of Beachfront High with his hood up and music blasting in his ears. He reached his locker and grabbed what he needed after putting away what he didn't as quickly as he could. He was hoping to avoid Dumb and Dumber.

Unfortunately, he wasn't that lucky.

Even as Fox took out his earbuds, he groaned as two familiar voices rang out.

"Hey, Kitty!" Dumb yelled.

Fox growled.

"Good morning Kitty Cat! Got my homework done and ready? Coach says I need to keep up my grades or I'll lose my scholarship!" Dumb said.

"Oh no! That would be a tragedy! To lose your scholarship due to your own stupidity!" Fox said dramatically and dripped with sarcasm.

"Hey! I'm not stupid! Just too busy to do my own homework, Kitty," Dumb replied.

"One, my name is Fox. Two, how will you learn if you don't do your own homework? Three, foxes are canines, not felines, dipshit."

"Canines and felines are the same, duh," Dumber sneered.

"How the fuck did you pass kindergarten?" Fox asked with a raised eyebrow.

"What does that have to do with anything?" Dumber asked.

Fox rolled his eyes, wanting to facepalm. Instead, he pasted a sickly sweet smirk on his face. "Dogs are canines and cats are felines. If you did your own homework, you would know that."

The bullies sputtered as they tried to come up with something to say back to him. Fox snickered, then turned to his locker and grabbed his books and sketch pad and then headed to class when the bullies called out to him.

"Get back here bitch! We ain't done!" Dumb demanded.

A teacher poked his head out of the classroom with an irritated scowl. He heard the commotion going on between the boys, and he knew which ones were causing problems.

"Mr. Valdez and Mr. Narus, is there a problem?"

"No sir, no problem," Fox said. "Alex and Baxter here just needed to know the time. We'll be heading to class now."

Fox turned away and headed up a flight of stairs to the second floor. His first class was a study hall in which he usually slept or drew rough sketches for Cyanide, his comic. He arrived at the classroom and took his seat at the front desk on the far left of the room. He dug out his sketch pad and got busy. Fox became so wrapped up in his comic that he jumped when he felt a hand on his shoulder and heard the teacher speaking.

"That's a spooky-looking beast. A wolf skeleton with only some fur covering the body is what I'm guessing. Is he the villain to your hero?" she asked.

Fox stared at his study hall teacher for a moment. She smiled at him.

"Sorry. I can see you're drawing a rough draft. Is it a comic page or strip?" she asked sheepishly.

Fox snapped out of his moment of disbelief and smiled back.

"Page, actually, and it's an anti-hero," Fox said, happy to talk about his work.

"It?" the teacher asked, confused but intrigued at the same time.

"Yeah. My anti-hero is neither male nor female. It is a corpse. Sure, it had a gender when it was alive, but since it's dead, it doesn't anymore," Fox explained. "To answer your next question, it was brought to life with necromancy."

"Necromancy? Fascinating. Since it was brought to life with magic does it serve a master or mistress?"

"It had a master but became self-aware due to the soul inside of it. It decided to rebel and do its own thing rather than listen to a human."

"Well. Very interesting. Are you publishing your work?" she asked.

Fox was stunned into silence for a moment. He never thought of publishing his work. He wouldn't know where to start.

"Publish, ma'am?" he asked.

"Sure. It seems you have a knack for story-telling, you should really consider it," she said with a smile. "Who knows, you could become the next Stan Lee."

Fox smirked slyly and asked, "Are you a Marvel fan?"

"I have a thing for Iron Man." She gave him a wink "Well, his suit anyway. The tech is stunning and revolutionary! I wish we had it. Tony Stark himself can suck it."

Fox laughed and found a new respect for his study hall teacher. After talking more about Marvel and what characters ruled and sucked, Fox went back to work on his rough draft. On the page, Cyanide was locked in battle with the crime syndicate, The Poison Lei. They used black magic to commit their crimes, which ranged from grave robbing to the most brutal of murders. They had done this for centuries, and Cyanide decided to be the one to put them down.

Fox's hand flew over the page, sketching scene after scene. Cyanide was struggling to escape but putting up a good fight. On the page, Cyanide sunk his skeletal claw into one of the Poison Lei member's chests and yanked out their heart, throwing it to the Head Mistress' feet.

The bell rang just as Fox finished the page. He packed up his stuff and headed out to his most hated class, Arithmetic. Algebra and Geometry he understood, but Arithmetic? What in the fresh hell is that nonsense about? Fox was thankful for online tutors.

Episode 2

Lunch, a time where Fox could just relax and continue to doodle to his little heart's content, or until the bell rang. He had a spot underneath a giant palm tree. The shade was nice, plus the breeze was a bonus.

Fox scratched his head as he was trying to figure out this page. It had been giving him trouble and he wasn't sure where to go with it. Cyanide had escaped the Poison Lei and was now in hiding, but that's where he seemed to be stuck. What should Cyanide do next? Something at that point in the story was rubbing him the wrong way. He stared at the rough sketch in his lap. Cyanide was lying in a cave, which was bad for him, but he was recovering from his escape.

Fox's own little brand of Spidey Sense went off when he heard the crunch of grass beneath the person's feet as they approached. They stopped right in front of him and he looked up. There before him was a bleach blonde vixen.

"Sorry mate, but you mind if I chill for a spell next to ya? It's pretty packed inside the mess hall and it's a lovely day," she said with a bright smile.

Fox fought the urge to sigh and nodded. The girl smiled bigger and sat next to him as she fished her lunch bag out of her cupcake-themed knapsack. She took out a doughnut-themed lunch bag and opened it, and then pulled out a sandwich, unwrapped it and took a huge bite. The blonde turned to Fox and held out her sandwich to him.

"Ya f'a'cy o'bi?" she mumbled around the bite she had in her mouth.

"No, but thank you," Fox said politely.

She shrugged and finished off her sandwich in three bites.

"Ah. Chipped chopped ham and cheese. My fave." The girl moaned in pleasure. She let out a burp that would make a sailor blush. She blushed herself and looked at a surprised Fox and smiled sheepishly, "Sorry mate. I was starving."

Fox shook his head and dismissed it. "So, where are you from? You're not from around here that's for sure."

"Got it one, mate. I come from *the land down under*," she sang the last part.

Fox pretended to drum on beer bottles while humming, making the blonde laugh. After the two shared a giggle, Fox asked his next question.

"Which part are you from?"

"Good Ol' Sydney! Moved here after my parents divorced. What about you, mate? Are you from here? You don't seem like it."

"I was born here but my parents are from the mainland," he said. "I'm Fox, by the way. Fox Kane."

"Nice to meet you, Fox. I'm Samantha Gray, though if you would lift your head from your drawing pad once in a while, you would know that," Samantha said with a giggle.

Fox looked at her, confused. Samantha laughed.

"We're in a bunch of classes together you knucklehead. You're either busy sleeping or doodling," she said, still laughing a bit.

Fox snorted then said, with loving snark, "I'm a lone wolf and my doodling is practice. Practice makes perfect."

Samantha laughed again and shook her head. "You're a funny one. Well, Mr. Artist, we have Calculus next. Care to escort a lovely lady to class?"

Fox rolled his eyes playfully and got up from the ground. He dusted himself off, packed up his stuff as Samantha did the same, and escorted her to their next class.

The day passed relatively slow, but then again, to Fox, Thursdays were slow days. The final bell rang, and Fox headed for home. He took the long way as he was in no rush.

Fox walked down the street of a neighborhood that most people tended to avoid, and for good reasons. He smiled, hearing the sound of chickens, and walked up to a gate. He looked down and saw baby chicks exploring the yard. He then looked up to see his elderly neighbor.

"Aloha Fox, how was school today?" she asked

"Aloha Doris. Same old same old," Fox said with a shrug.

"Are those hooligans bothering you?"

"Sadly, yeah. Most teachers don't do anything as that would mean punishing their golden football stars," Fox scoffed.

"Well, if that ain't a crock of shit then I must be old," Doris said with a scowl.

Fox laughed, "I don't know, Doris, those grey hairs tell me otherwise."

Fox ducked then watched as the chickens fought over the corn and chicken feed that Doris tried to throw at him. He laughed, but lost his smile as he looked back at the house behind him. He sighed.

"I better get inside," Fox said softly, with a hint of fear. "I have some homework and I want to start on my latest comic page."

Doris looked at the boy with a saddened gaze. She wished there was something she could do for him, but there really wasn't anything. The foster care system was so broken, a lot of children would remain where they are due to lack of evidence or end up somewhere worse.

"Go on, then. No need to make that man mad," she said softly.

Fox nodded then shuddered. This was one foster parent that honestly scared him.

"Yeah. Aloha Doris," Fox said.

"Aloha dear," she said back.

Fox gulped, turned and walked over to the dreaded place. He entered the house across the street from Doris then bolted up the stairs. Making it to the hallway, he flinched as an angry voice boomed.

"Fox! Where you at boy?"

Fox didn't hesitate and took off down the hall to the room at the far left end. He ran in and slammed the door shut. He pushed his dresser in front of the door, barricading it. He jumped when his foster father pounded on the door.

"Fox! You open this door boy!"

SLAM SLAM SLAM SLAM!

The more he pounded, the closer Fox got to hyperventilating.

"Please leave, please leave, please leave!" Fox whispered to himself.

SLAM SLAM SLAM SLAM!

Mike pounded and screamed for several more minutes before leaving. Silence filled the air until Fox heard the sound of a truck belonging to the man turn over and roar as he left.

Fox shook as he got up and collapsed on his bed. He closed his eyes and tried to calm his racing heart.

He looked over at his door and decided to leave it alone for now. He felt safer with the barricade and laid back down to fall into a restless sleep.

Episode 3

Fox jerked awake and gasped for breath. He looked around the room and then toward the door. He sighed and remembered what happened. He was no stranger to nightmares, especially after Mike does that or worse to him. He rubbed his eyes and stretched. Fox grabbed his phone and saw that it was midnight! He'd been asleep since three in the afternoon. Then again, with Mike, sleep was elusive.

He pushed the dresser aside then silently made his way downstairs to the kitchen. Opening the fridge, he took out a slice of pizza and wolfed it down. He didn't care that it was cold since he didn't want to run the risk of waking Mike if he was home and sleeping off his latest alcohol binge.

"Hey kiddo," a voice behind him said softly.

Fox startled, nearly jumping out his skin, still on edge from earlier. He turned to find his foster sister standing in the kitchen doorway. He groaned. The girl was a foot taller than him and she was muscular probably from her job. She had long black hair tied up in a bun, chocolate eyes, and she wore scrubs.

"Thanks for the heart attack, Alice," he deadpanned.

"You're welcome," she teased.

The two stood in silence for a few moments before Alice broke it.

"Are you okay?"

"Yeah," Fox said.

"Bullshit." Alice gave him her 'mom' look.

Fox shrugged and changed the subject. Not wanting to worry the one person who actually took care of him other than Doris.

"Heading to work?" he asked.

"Yup. I have a double shift tonight, so I can't take you to school tomorrow."

"S'okay. I can take care of myself," Fox said with a smile.

"Sure," Alice said sarcastically.

"Hey!"

Alice giggled, "All right, I gotta go. I have patients to look after and horny doctors to keep off my ass."

"Like any doctor wants your ass," Fox snorts.

Alice whacked him on the head lovingly and then hugged him goodnight. She kissed the top of his head and left for work. Fox sighed and headed back to his room.

He finished the cold slice of pizza he had been munching on and changed into his sleep clothes. He would do his homework in his morning study hall class and his comic strip later. He risked a trip to the bathroom to get ready for bed. He did it in record time and rushed back to the room as quietly as he could, then locked the door behind him. He fell back into a restless sleep, then an all too familiar nightmare took hold of him.

Six-year-old Fox whimpers as the storm rages on outside. The thunder booms and lightning flashes lighting up the dark home in an eerie way. Little Fox gets out of bed and heads down the hallway to the winding staircase.

"Mommy?" Fox calls out.

There is no answer, so little Fox decides to head downstairs to investigate. He carefully makes his way down to the bottom and to the main foyer then goes to the living room. Not seeing his mother, he treks to the kitchen and whimpers. She isn't there either.

He looks through the glass door leading out to his beach backyard. Lightning flashes and illuminates a figure that was standing right behind the door. Fox screams as he spots the demonic-looking wolf.

"MOMMY!"

Fox bolted up and gasped for breath. He looked around to see if the creature was lurking about and sighed in relief when he didn't spot it. He took one more glance around the room to be sure he was awake and safe. He gulped in a few deep breaths to calm his racing heart and ran a hand through his short blonde spiked hair.

"Geez, Mother. What the fuck were you into? I know that night was no dream," Fox muttered to himself.

He took another deep breath then looked at his phone to see what time it was. He groaned when he saw he needed to get up and get ready for school. He grabbed a clean pair of boxers, jeans, and a gray v-neck tee-shirt then headed for the bathroom. Fox quickly peeked out the window and sighed in relief. Mike's truck was gone.

Fox quickly showered and dressed, brushed his teeth, spiked his hair, rushed back to his room and grabbed his school bag, he put on his boots and hurried out the door to run the three miles to school.

"It's a good thing I live on a small island where three miles is three blocks," Fox said to himself, panting for breath. "God, I'm in poor shape for seventeen."

Fox made it to school just in time for the first bell and walked to his locker. He grabbed what he needed and headed to his study hall. He did his homework from last night and checked it over. Satisfied with his work, he pulled out his sketch pad and began doodling. As usual. The morning passed and Fox found himself in his favorite class. Art. Surprise, surprise. He walked in and smirked.

"Ah! My young artist has arrived!" his teacher exclaimed happily.

Fox took a bow, smiling. "Thank you, thank you! I'd like to thank my muse for being so awesome."

The amused art teacher took his own bow. "All right, you. Grab your masterpiece and a palette." He clapped his hands. "Let's get to work, people!"

Fox chuckled and along with his fellow classmates, he grabbed his painting and supplies then took a seat at an easel. He placed his painting on the easel, got his supplies set up. He then got to work. Fox dipped his brush into some paint and began stroking the canvas. He never really liked the texture of canvases and was glad his teacher had Gesso on hand. Gesso made the canvas smooth and allowed different colors to show up in different hues. A few minutes went by and his art teacher was suddenly behind him with a dreamy look on his face.

"This is truly your best work, Fox." Mr. Danic sighed.

Fox snorted a laugh. "Are you sure you should be an art teacher and not a drama teacher?"

Mr. Danic let out a *HA* and flipped his shoulder-length hair back.

"Drama is for little girls with nothing to do but whine on the internet about their silly celebrity crush," he said. "Art is life! Life to be seen, to be created. A bold passion."

Fox nearly failed at holding back his laughter. "If you say so," he said.

"Honestly though, Mr. Kane, this painting of yours is quite the masterpiece. If you don't mind, I'd like to save it for my seniors next year," Mr. Danic said.

Fox was shocked but thrilled at the same time. He didn't show off his work often, but was always happy when he got the chance. He was also happy someone loved his art.

"I'm cool with it," he said with a bright smile.

"Excellent! I really do love it, Fox. You've captured a moment so brilliantly. You can sense the terror of the little one and yet see the elegance of the storm as it illuminates the nightmare haunting the poor child."

Mr. Danic moved away to check on the other students and Fox got back to work. The painting was truly haunting yet elegant at the same time, as the instructor said. The scene showed a child in a dark kitchen with lightning lighting up the room and the horrific creature that lurked outside. An all too real fever dream that was forever burned into his mind. Fox shuddered and continued to paint.

Episode 4

The end of the day came by the sound of the bell ringing to tell students they were free. Fox walked out of the building then headed down a familiar road he hadn't been on in a long, long time. He was not too fond of the idea of going home. so he made a side trip and stopped in front of the house he had not thought of in years.

He startled when a pair of hands suddenly blocked his vision. Tensed and ready for a fight, Fox prepared himself when he heard a giggle.

"Guess who?" a voice asked.

"Hmm. I don't know. A stalker?" Fox asked.

Samantha removed her hands with a laugh and danced, her white flowing skirt twirling perfectly with her movement, and then stood in front of Fox. She crossed her arms behind her back, her fingers fiddling with the hem of her sky blue cami shirt. She then moved her fingers to play with the top of her thigh-high black boots.

"As if, mate! But I am curious as to why you were walking down this way by your lonesome," she said.

Fox looked at Samantha, then his old childhood home. He sighed heavily. "I used to live here."

Samantha looked at Fox with curiosity. "Oh? A childhood home?"

Fox nodded and tried to swallow past the lump in his throat. He wondered briefly if he should tell Samantha about his past, and inwardly shook his head. He decided to reveal only a little.

"I lived here with my Mom. Like your parents, they were separated, but unlike your parents, mine were never married."

"Really?" Samantha asked, surprised. "It's not unheard of but certainly not the norm. I mean, most couples get married eventually." Growing up, she was positive that most couples got married sometime down the road.

Fox shrugged. "Really. I'm not sure why they didn't marry, but they had their reasons."

Samantha nodded and motioned for Fox to continue.

"My Mom and I lived here while my Dad was back on the mainland. According to her, he was living in Nevada at the time. After I turned six, my Dad found out where we were and he came here. One night I heard them arguing along with gunshots and then silence," Fox said softly, with a slight tremor in his voice.

Samantha looked at him with a mix of emotions but couldn't say anything as she put the pieces of the puzzle together. After a brief moment of silence, Samantha found her voice. "So, you're a foster child?"

"Yeah. Not for much longer though. When I turn eighteen, I'll inherit the money my mother left me and this house."

Samantha looked at Fox like he grew two heads, "How do you know?"

"Easy. She made a will before I was born and left everything to me. I found the document after breaking into a computer when I was left in the care of a lawyer. I overheard him say he found something on my mother in the archives and that is when I got curious and found the will," he said matter-of-factly. "I was about twelve at the time. My foster brother was a hacker and showed me how to get into his dad's computer."

Samantha couldn't believe what she was hearing but somehow she knew it was the truth.

"So this gorgeous home will be yours?" She waved her hand towards the house.

"Yeah, in about two weeks," Fox said with a mix of relief and fear in his voice.

Samantha looked at Fox confused. She understood why he would be relieved. From what she heard, the American foster system was a mess and many children suffer because of it. Hell, she heard some children don't survive long in the care of their foster parents. She shuddered at that thought. The fear, however, she didn't know what that was about. Not wanting to dwell on it any longer, she closed her eyes and put it out of her mind. She reopened them after taking a deep breath.

Samantha looked at the beautiful home and was suddenly curious as to what it looks like on the inside.

She looked over to Fox and found him on the porch already peering through the large window as if he was studying something. She watched as he picked the lock and headed inside. She squeaked quietly and ran up behind him.

No way was she staying outside when there was something in front of her to be explored!

Episode 5

Fox walked into the foyer with Samantha behind him. He tried the light switch on the wall by the door and was surprised when the lights came on.

Fox looked over to Samantha and she shrugged with a confused look. He then took note of the symbols by the door. Samantha noticed them as well.

"What are those?" she asked, staring at the symbols on the walls.

"They're sigils," Fox said.

He walked up to the wall and placed his hand over one of the markings. He never noticed these or if he did, he didn't remember them being there.

"Sigils? For protection?" she asked.

"Something like that," Fox joked. "Huh?"

"What?"

"These look like they were placed here recently. They don't look aged or anything," Fox said.

Samantha agreed with that. They did look like they were drawn there not too long ago. She then headed into the kitchen to see if there were more drawings around the back door when a shadow passed by. She shuddered and shrugged it off as her mind playing tricks on her. Fox trailed behind her, finding a light switch and flicking on the lights. Fox turned on the tap and was shocked to find the water was still on.

"What the hell? Running water and the lights still work? How? They should've been turned off years ago."

Samantha shrugged and looked through the cabinets to see if there was something hiding within. She looked back at Fox to find he was gone.

"Fox?"

"Upstairs!" he called back to her.

"You all right?"

"Fine! You find anything?"

"No! Every cubby is empty!"

"Search the living room and the den! Maybe there's something there!"

"I'm on it!"

Samantha headed into the living room to search first, since it was fairly large. She hoped Fox was okay upstairs.

Fox took in a deep breath and wandered down the hallway. The first two rooms were an office and guest room. A guest bathroom was next, then the last two bedrooms were Fox's old room and his mother's room. Fox headed to his room first and peered inside. Like the home, it had been untouched and not a speck of dust in sight.

Fox should've been freaking out at least a little by all this but couldn't rise above the confusion. A shadow slinked by, and he followed it to the office.

Fox walked into the office and felt off. Like something was here but he couldn't see anything out of place. He looked around and found a book on the bookshelf that screamed at him to look inside.

He picked it up and read it, or at least tried to.

"What nonsense is this? Latin?" Fox wondered out loud.

He flipped through the pages, and a saved page with the corner dogged eared caught his eye.

Back downstairs, Samantha searched the den after not finding much in the living room. She looked at the books on the shelf in the corner of the room and sighed. Nothing. She was about to place the book she had back on the shelf when something fell out of it. She picked up the piece of paper and read it. She bolted up the stairs with the paper clutched in her hand.

"Fox?" she called down the hall.

"In the office! First door on the left!"

She raced into the room and took a moment to catch her breath. Then she straightened up and handed him the paper she found. Fox took it and read it over. Samantha watched as an array of emotions swept over his face.

"You okay, mate?"

"Where did you find this?" he asked in a low tone, ignoring her question.

Samantha looked at Fox with concern. "Down in the den. I was looking through the books and found one out of place. I was putting it back when this slipped out."

Fox raced out of the room and down the winding stairs, heading into the den. He scanned the bookshelf, finding the book that Samantha mentioned resting on the shelf, Fox picked it up. He flipped through the book and found nothing else. He heard Samantha coming into the room.

"Fox, are you all right?"

"How in the ever-living fuck did this get here?" he asked, more to himself than her.

"I don't know, maybe your Mom had it for a reason," Samantha said, trying to soothe him.

Fox shook his head vigorously, "How? She and my Dad died on the same night. Hell, they died together! How did she get a police report of my father's death?"

"I don't know. The report says your father's body went missing from the morgue that night. Maybe he's alive and planted it here."

Fox heard her nervous tone and stared at her for a minute before looking away. His memories told him that his father died that night. He bit the knuckle of his index finger.

"It has to be fake. I know he's dead," he said around his knuckle.

Samantha tried to say something to him, but Fox only nodded and sighed as he took in this bit of info. He nearly jumped out of his skin when Samantha hugged him. He hesitated and lightly hugged back for a minute before letting her go. He looked away from her and headed back upstairs with her trailing behind. He went back into the office and picked up the book he was reading before Samantha came in.

"What's that?" she asked.

"Not sure. It's a book, obviously," he said with some sarcasm. "But I can't read it. It seems to be in Latin."

Samantha rolled her eyes, hearing the sarcasm in his voice. "And you know this how?"

"Because I lived with a priest for a few months, and he taught me a little bit of it, but I'm not fluent,"

"Can you read any of this?"

Fox nodded. "I can make out a few words. Like this one, necromantia. It's necromancy."

"Necromancy? As in bringing the dead back to life?" Samantha asked with a shudder.

He gave her another nod, "Yup. Necromancy is a very dark spell. You never mess with the dead."

Samantha nodded and noticed scribbling on the side of the page. "There's something handwritten here."

Fox looked at the page. He had never seen it before, but assumed it was his mother's handwriting. He wasn't able to tell what the worn out writing stated.

"Any idea on what it says?" Samantha asked.

"No. The page is too old and it seems my mother had the type of handwriting that is impossible to read," Fox said with a groan.

"Like a doctor."

Fox looked at her with annoyance, but was still amused so he snorted then laughed when Samantha punched him in the arm.

"Well, what are we standing around for? Let's get to work, yeah?" she asked with a smile.

Fox returned the smile and sat at the desk, while Samantha pulled a chair closer. They got to work trying to piece this puzzle together.

Episode 6

Fox and Samantha had been hard at work for what seemed like hours, and they came up with nothing. He took a look at his phone and sighed. It was getting late and he knew he should head home, but he didn't want to. Plus, he wanted to translate the book in his arm, and with the power still being on, he could use the desktop computer on the desk to do research.

Samantha pulled out her own phone with a yawn, and checked for messages. "Goodness me, it's late isn't it?"

"Yeah. You should probably head home. I wouldn't want your father to get worried and come looking for you," Fox said.

"I should, but I want to stay as well. I want to help crack the mystery of this book and those sigils downstairs," Samantha said, stretching after sitting in the chair for so long.

"I forgot about those for a moment. Mental note made, but anyways you should really head home. I'll be all right."

"You're going to spend the night?"

Fox nodded. He didn't want to say the real reason why he was staying, but she figured it out or at least part of it. He saw that look in her eye. The look that she just read him like an open book.

With a soft tone you would use with frightened animals, she said, "You don't want to go home?"

Fox didn't look at her. Silence washed over them for a moment, and Samantha came to a realization. He looked out the window and stared at the waves crashing on the beach.

With the same soft tone, "You're being abused, aren't you?"

Fox shrugged. It wasn't like he hadn't been abused before. This was nothing. He was fine.

"Fox! Why didn't you say anything? Or why don't you fight back or something?" Samantha demanded in concern and anger but not at Fox.

He waved her off, "Calm down. I'll be eighteen in two weeks remember? I'll be able to move out then. Besides we only just met, why are you so worried?"

"Still. My father has a really great lawyer. We could've gotten you some help. You don't have to be abused by your foster mum and dad." Samantha crossed her arms over her chest.

"Foster dad, actually. The mother died before I was taken in," Fox said.

"Oh. Do you know what happened to her?"

Fox took in a deep breath and exhaled. It wasn't his story to tell, but he figured Samantha was the type to try and get information in her own way. "According to my foster sister, she committed suicide. She didn't go into details as she doesn't actually know how or why her mother did it, but suspects it was an overdose. My sister also says there were no signs or warnings. She just woke up one morning and found her mother's body in the bathroom."

Samantha brought her hands up to her mouth and covered it, horrified; she removed her hands after a moment and exclaimed, "That's awful! The husband didn't help her, at all?!"

"He apparently doesn't believe in mental illnesses," Fox spat with a disgusted tone.

"Sick fuck!" Samantha hissed angrily.

Fox nodded, not really wanting to talk about it any further. Luckily for him, Samantha got the hint and dropped the subject. For now, at least.

"You sure you'll be all right here for the night?" Samantha asked in concern.

"Mommy, wow, I'm a big boy now," Fox snarked.

Samantha punched his arm with a laugh. "Smartass. All right then. I best head home before my father decides to send a search party."

Fox waved her off and was shocked when she hugged him again and kissed his cheek. She waved and headed out the door, leaving Fox alone in the big empty house.

He shook himself off and snapped out of it. He told himself he had no time to think or dwell on what just happened, and he needed to get to work.

Fox went over to the desk with the book in his arms and set it down. He booted up the laptop. He swore when a lock screen popped up asking for a password.

"Of course. Why should anything be easy?"

Fox grumbled as he attempted to figure out the password. He tried his name, birthday, his parent's names and birthdays, and nothing. He flipped through the book and found a name or what he thought was a name. He typed in Poison Lei, and the lock screen opened. Fox winced as his Spidey sense went off for a moment. He made a mental note of that and went back to what he was doing. The desktop just had a picture of him and his mother when he was a baby. She was smiling brightly at the baby with her long wavy blonde hair framing her face.

Tears ran down Fox's face. He wiped them away, as he told himself he didn't have time for this. He opened the internet browser and got to work on translating the book.

Hours went by, and Fox started to get frustrated. The only thing he got was that the spell was necromancy, and another had been bookmarked to read after. He decided to take a break and went downstairs. He went into the den and scanned the bookshelf looking for an answer. The laptop on the desk was dead and wouldn't turn on.

"Fan-fucking-tastic!" He exclaimed.

Fox turned to head upstairs when something caught his eye. A light shone from a crack in the wall. He went back up to the bookcase and felt the wall. He moved the bookcase away from the wall and kicked it in, revealing a room. He stepped inside and found the light switch which was glued into the upward position keeping the light on. Fox looked around and found an altar.

"What in the name of everything is this?"

The table had a bowl with candles surrounding it being guarded with protection sigils and runes. Fox looked around the small room, then found a cabinet filled with herbs and other objects for spell casting. The room was also decorated with moon and star charts. The walls were a basic white with the rest of the house being painted with dark blues and grays.

A shiver crawled down his spine. The room gave him the creeps.

Fox cautiously looked into the bowl on the table and found nothing inside. It was empty and strangely clean, not a speck of dust like the rest of the home. Fox took the bowl and candles out of the room and upstairs with him. He placed the objects on the floor setting them up as they were back in the room.

"What the fuck am I doing? Am I really going to see if magic exists?" He sucked in a sharp, deep breath. "Yeah, I am. Curiosity with a mix of insanity."

He grabbed the book and flipped through it a few items. He tried to read some of the Latin and went from what he knew, then tried to speak words from the scribbles even though he really couldn't.

Fox grabbed his bag and pulled out a fully colored drawing of his anti-hero, Cyanide. He placed it in the bowl, then poured in ink from a pod he used to draw the ink beast in his comics to replace his sanguis, the Latin word for blood. Fox lit the candles and began chanting the best he could, but knew he was butchering some of the words, then read the next spell he found.

Fox waited for a few moments before huffing a sigh and putting the book down.

He scoffed. "So magic isn't real. Surprise, surprise. Jeez, mother what the fuck were you into?"

He cleaned his mess and grabbed a wallet out of the backpack. He headed down the winding staircase and out the front door not bothering to lock it as he was coming right back. He jogged down the street the way he came and headed for a small twenty four-hour diner on the corner of the street, about five blocks on the right side. His school was only two blocks away but he had no intention of going there at night as some gangs and dealers hung out there after hours. Fox went into the diner and ordered a cheeseburger meal to go.

The elderly waitress looked at him concerned. "Are you all right Ku'uipo? You look pale," she asked.

He looked at the waitress, confused, and spotted himself in the mirror that was hanging on the wall behind her. She was right. He was pale, but wasn't sure how he got that way. He smiled regardless and waved it off. He felt fine.

"Maika'i no au, mahalo," Fox said cheerfully.

The waitress still looked concerned but accepted the answer. "All right. Your order will be ready in a few."

Fox nodded, then grabbed the newspaper someone left on the counter nearby and began to read. There wasn't much in the news except a story about a corrupt politician on the mainland getting arrested. Fox shook his head.

"There's always one, isn't there?" he muttered to himself.

Fox paid for his order when it was ready. He jogged back to the house, sat at the island counter in the kitchen, and dug in with gusto. After he was finished, he headed back upstairs to the office. Since he wasn't able to translate the book, he decided to try and see what the sigils mean.

"They must be for protection, but something tells me there's more to them than that," Fox wondered aloud.

He typed away and found an answer a few hours later, but was too tired to think straight and saved his pages. He then laid down on the couch by the window and fell into a restless sleep.

Episode 7

Fox tosses and turns in his bed and wakes up when thunder crashes loudly overhead. He sits up and notices he is in his old room.

Fox looks around, confused, and his eyes land on the mirror upon the wall. He looks at himself, scared. He gets out of bed and walks up to the glass. He is ashen and his veins are showing, but instead of the usual blue color, they are black.

He panics. "What the fuck? What is this? What's happening to me?"

A growling sound answers him and Fox jumps back, looking around in a panicked haze. He looks in the mirror and the blackness has spread.

Fox races to the bathroom and turns on the shower getting in. He scrubs his body, hoping to get the blackness off, but it continues to spread. The growling sound grows louder and his heart races.

He stumbles out of the shower, panting, and looks in the mirror once more. The blackness covered his whole body, then his skin begins to slowly decay away, revealing his skeleton underneath.

He screams in pain and fear. "What's happening to me? What the fuck is this?"

The transformation reaches completion and, as the pain subsides, the house goes quiet. The skeletal creature looks into the mirror and finds a demonic looking beast! The skeleton was that of a wolf and the black patches that hang from his bones were ink. The spells worked. Fox steps back in fear and howls.

Fox bolted up, panting as if he just ran a marathon. He rushed to the guest bathroom and looked in the mirror. His eyes were glazed over and he still looked ashen.

"It had to be a dream. It had to be," he said confused.

Fox jumped when the door opened and a voice called out. He sighed as he recognized it as Samantha's.

"Fox? Are you up? I have breakfast! Rather brunch since it's also lunchtime!"

He hesitated, then answered, "I'm up! I'm coming!"

Fox rushed back into the office and grabbed a spare set of clothes he kept in his bag, just in case, and quickly changed. He headed downstairs and joined Samantha at the island table, then found grocery bags sitting on the counter by the sink and stove. She was putting things away in cabinets and the fridge.

"What's all this?" he asked.

Samantha turned around from the grocery bags she was organizing and gasped at the sight of Fox.

"Are you all right? Do you need a hospital?" she asked, panicked.

Fox was confused, and then it hit him. The spells.

"I might've tried the you-know-what last night and this is the outcome," he said sheepishly.

"Are you mad? What if you're dying right now?" Samantha shouted.

Fox raised his hands in a surrender pose. "Not dying. I feel fine. Please calm down and tell me what you brought."

Samantha glared at him, hoping she'd break him, but failed. "Fine. We will talk about it."

Fox nodded, with no intention of finishing the conversation. Samantha gave a nod back and changed the subject for the time being.

"Before I left last night, I took a quick peek in the fridge and cupboards and found them empty. So I did a little shopping for you. Luckily the grocery store near my house is open pretty early in the morning." She smiled.

Fox looked at her with a mixture of confusion and gratitude.

"Thanks," he said softly.

Samantha gave him a megawatt smile. "You're very welcome, mate! There's some plastic ware, cups, and plates along with spoons and forks. I also got you some shower stuff, I imagine you need some, and I brought some clothes that Father never wears anymore, so don't worry, he won't even notice they're gone."

Fox looked at Samantha with more gratitude and less confusion.

"You know I have to go home eventually, right? It's Saturday and we have school on Monday."

Samantha lost her smile, "I know. But I figured you'd spend the weekend here and then slowly move in after."

Fox nodded and hungrily eyed the McDonalds bag on the counter. "What's for breakfast?"

Samantha's smile returned and she pushed it toward him. "I brought some hash browns, egg and cheese McMuffins, along with sausage if you don't like eggs, and hotcakes. Dig in!"

Fox did not need to be told twice. He grabbed a container of hotcakes with a sausage McMuffin along with a hash brown. The two ate breakfast in silence and then cleaned up their mess.

Samantha broke the silence first. "Did you find out what the sigils mean or translate the book?"

Fox groaned. "I for the life of me could not translate that damn thing. I did recognize some of the words, but I'm pretty sure I butchered the spells."

"Spells? More than one?" Samantha asked, confused.

He nodded. "The necromancy spell was first, then there's another spell that I couldn't make out."

"And you still performed them?" She raised her voice.

"Stop shouting. My curiosity got the better of me. If this is a side effect, I'm sure it'll wear off soon," Fox said calmly.

Samantha decided to shrug it off for now and change the subject. "Did you ever find out what the sigils by the door mean?"

"I found the answer but I was too tired to look, so I went to bed shortly after. I saved the page so we can take a look now," Fox said.

Samantha nodded and followed Fox upstairs to the office. He booted up the laptop and brought up the saved pages.

"From what this says, the sigils are for protection, but they're also magic sigils. Two of them are for protection, the other two are time stoppers," Fox explained.

Samantha looked at Fox like he had escaped the mental ward.

"Tell me I heard that right, mate," she said.

"You heard right, mate. North and South are for protection, East and West are to stop time. That's why the house looks untouched and why the water and electricity is still on. Time stops when the house is empty and flows when it's not. The protection sigils are designed to keep anything and everything evil out," Fox said tiredly.

"Huh. It doesn't make sense. Like, at all," Samantha said, staring at the computer screen.

He chuckled. "Welcome to the world of magic. Nothing makes sense, like sports."

Samantha snorted and read over the research then shook her head. She was still worried about his ashen complexion and decided he needed some sun. She shut the laptop and dragged him outside.

"What are we doing out here?" Fox asked, a bit antsy.

"Going for a walk. Duh."

"Why?" he said with a sigh.

"Because you need a little break and some sun. Now stop whining like a sheila whose Aunt Flow is visiting," she teased.

Fox looked at Samantha like she had turned green with bright polka dots, but shrugged and decided a walk might just be what the doctor ordered. Plus, he hadn't walked on the beach in a long time. The beach was empty, since it was a private one. The ocean was a beautiful blue and green color, and the sound of the waves were calming. The two walked along the white sand until they hit a small cove. Palm trees swayed gently in the warm breeze, seemingly waving at them, inviting them to come in. They looked at each other and decided to explore. They found a cave off the right side of the cove and headed inside, Samantha leading with her phone's flashlight. The two noticed writing and drawings on the walls of the cave.

"Look at these symbols and writing. Do you think a cult used to be here?" Samantha asked.

Fox wondered the same as he examined them. He noticed a picture of a lei with the word *'poison'* next to it. Fox was confused. The only poison lei he knew of was the crime syndicate in his comics. He racked his brains and remembered seeing the picture in several of his dreams.

"It can't be," Fox whispered to himself.

Samantha looked at Fox in concern, and it deepened when she saw that knowing look on his face. "You all right, mate?"

"Fine," he said in a monotone voice.

"Does that picture remind you of something?" she asked.

"It's just...In my comics, Cyanide fights an underground crime syndicate that wants to use him, called The Poisoned Lei. I came up with it when I kept seeing this picture over and over in my dreams."

"Bit of an odd coincidence," Samantha said.

"That's the thing. I don't think this is a coincidence."

"Are you saying your comics have come to life?" she asked, looking at Fox like he was a mental case.

"Not to life. I think they already existed. I mean, in my dreams I saw a demonic skeletal wolf thing that I based my character off of and The Poisoned Lei off of a picture. What if my mother was a part of some cult and what I saw when I was little was real and not a dream?"

Samantha looked at Fox and then back to the wall. He was getting closer to the truth and it made her nervous.

"It could be a possibility. After all, there's always more to a story. Plus, you've been in the foster care system since you were six years old. What do you know about your mother?" Samantha asked.

Fox's thoughts came to a screeching halt. Samantha was right. There's always more to a story, but more than that was he didn't really know his mother at all. Nor his father. For all he knew one or both could have been in this cult and this group ended their lives. Could it be that or could it be something else just as evil.

"Guess I have more research to do," he wearily said.

"You know I'm always here to help if you need it," Samantha said sympathetically.

"Thanks, but I need to discover everything for myself."

Samantha nodded and knew he was right, but there was no reason she couldn't be there for him.

"I think I'm ready to head back. This place gives me the creeps," She shivered a little.

Fox gave her a sign of agreement, and the two headed back to the house. Fox sighed, he knew he needed to look around his soon to be home for more answers.

Samantha pulled on her sandals and sighed too. She didn't want to go home just yet, but she needed to as she had plans.

"I have to get home now. I have a dinner date with my Dad tonight. Well, it's more like him having a business dinner with his firm but taking me along for the ride," she said with a groan.

Fox snorted in amusement and told her, "Go, have fun. Tell me all about it on Monday."

"Monday?"

"I think you need a break from all this crazy, whatever it is. Take Daddy's credit card and go on a shopping spree or something," he said with a smirk.

"Smartass. I have my own credit card. I don't need Daddy's money. Though, I will take you up on that offer. I have a friend coming in tomorrow and I do want to be there to see him."

Fox nodded and walked her out to her car. He tensed up when she hugged him and pecked his cheek. She waved and headed out the door, leaving Fox to his own devices.

He went back up to the office and sat back at the desk, deciding to see if there could be something hidden on the laptop that could give Fox anything on his parents or the picture on the cave wall. He searched until the sun went down and he got frustrated.

He stretched and grabbed his wallet then headed back to the Mom and Pop diner he went to last night. The waitress was happy to see him again. She had been worried about him since she last saw him, and like Samantha, she was ready to call an ambulance when she saw his ashen face. He got the same thing as last night and headed home when it was ready.

After Fox ate his dinner, he decided to draw. He grabbed his sketch pad and art supplies, then went to the living room and sat on the couch. He sketched away bringing Cyanide to life in his adventure. He sketched until he got tired. He showered. He then changed into clean pajamas that Samantha brought and slept in his mother's room.

A low growl sounded in the room, but didn't wake him.

Episode 8

Fox hears the low growl and follows it through the darkness. The growls got louder and louder until he came to a beach. It's dark, with the only light being the moon. Something shifts in the dark and Fox looks around.

"Who's there?" he calls out.

Something moves again and Fox again demands it to reveal itself.

"Who's there? Reveal yourself!" Fox shouts.

"You know who I am," a growling demonic voice said.

"Do I? Come out and show me!"

"You do. You created me," the voice said.

"What do you mean I created you? Just come out already!" Fox demands again, getting angry and impatient.

"As you wish."

The thing steps into the moonlight, and Fox is shocked. It was him! His ink beast.

"Cyanide?" Fox asked, his voice shook.

The creature nodded. "Yes. You created me first on paper, then brought me to life with the spells. The last spell binds us together. We are one."

Fox stands there, shocked. Cyanide was here. He looks just as he'd drawn it in the comics: menacing, dull yellow bones with black veins, ink-like skin making him seem more creepy than cartoonish, hollow eye sockets with pinprick white dots for eyes, razor sharp teeth and claws. He stood on all four legs, though he could walk on two, black ink-like ears listening to their surroundings, and a long, skeletal tail. Fox should be terrified, but he isn't. Cyanide is his creation, after all.

"How are we one? If anything, the necromancy spell should've kept you separate from me and the binding incantation is just to keep you tethered to me," Fox explains.

"The spell was no ordinary binding one. It was a fusion contract. We are one," Cyanide said with a sinister laugh.

Before Fox could say anything, Cyanide lunged at him, and the two fused together. The creature howled to the moon.

"We're a new kind of Cyanide!" the two howl in unison.

Fox snapped awake and panted, as he tried to slow his pounding heart. He looked into the vanity mirror his mother had in her room and saw black inky veins had spread throughout, then vanished. His complexion turned back to a healthy tan.

"A new kind of Cyanide?" he asked, his voice shaking. He closed his eyes and flopped back onto the bed. "What's happening to my life?"

Fox looked at the clock on his phone and saw it was six in the morning. He groaned but got up and ready for the day, he then headed for the office to continue his search.

Elsewhere-Beachfront Airport

A man walked through the terminal of the local airport and spotted the girl he was meeting.

"Samantha," the man greeted when he walked up to her.

"Maddox. You took your bloody time getting here," Samantha said, not happy.

He scowled at her "I came as fast as I could."

"Come on then," she huffed. "We can't waste any more time."

"Who died and made you leader?" Maddox needed coffee because it was too bloody early for this.

"I've been promoted, or did you not get the memo?" Samantha growled.

Maddox grumbled as the two walked outside to the car waiting for them. They told the driver where to go and arrived at the hotel twenty minutes later. The building was gigantic and fairly busy. It was tourist season, after all. Reds and golds with spots of black and gray were the colors of the place. They could smell vanilla coming from the left at the breakfast bar. A large aquarium stood in the middle of the room showcasing various salt water fish, which they guessed were native to the island. They checked in at the front desk then headed for an elevator and rode it up to the fifth floor where they spotted their room and went inside.

"So, has he performed the spells yet?" Maddox asked.

Samantha nodded. "Aye. I'm not sure if it worked, though. Last I saw him, he was ashen like he was dying."

Maddox hummed and sorted out his weapons on the table in the room. There were knives of all sizes from a machete to a small hunting knife, and different guns like a simple glock to a small TMP. He smirked when he heard Samantha whistle.

"How the fuck did you get through customs, mate?" she asked.

"Magic," he said.

"Sure. We'll roll with that."

"Back to the subject at hand. Fox is ashen like he's dying? Have you seen him at all this morning?" Maddox asked, as he made mental notes.

"No. I came straight here. I'll be heading back to him shortly," Samantha said.

"Good. You remember the plan right?" Maddox gave her a hard look.

"Duh."

Maddox rolled his eyes at the childish answer. "A simple yes would have sufficed you know."

"Whatever. Are you sure you want to do this? This is your son after all. He's not even a part of them! I mean, didn't you say they all died out?"

"I did. In a raid gone wrong, the last generation of cultists was slaughtered by our organization. We thought they were all dead, my girlfriend included, but she somehow survived and was believed to be the last one until I found out she was pregnant. She fled here and stayed hidden. I found out where she was and put an end to her, leaving our son to live and grow up away from all that. Then this happened and I got your call and now I may have to put my own son down. I knew she would poison him eventually. Death will be his only release. I only hope the spells didn't work or we're not too late."

Samantha hoped the spells didn't work as well. She didn't want to see Fox get hurt or even killed. Not by the hands of his own father nonetheless, but something told her otherwise. She sighed and headed out to Fox's place.

In a weird, twisted way, she had come to like the boy. She may have even had a little crush on him.

"Fuck me if those spells worked," she whispered to herself.

Episode 9

Fox had already showered and dressed for the day. He rubbed his face and was thankful for his inability to grow a beard. He did wish that he would've gained some muscle and a six-pack like the superheroes he grew up with, but he was still a dollar twenty soaking wet and only five foot four.

"I have to be the scrawniest superhero. Anti-hero? Whatever. I have to be the boniest hero ever and the shortest," he muttered to himself as he posed in front of the mirror. He then splashed water on his face and shook his head. "I should be freaking out. Why aren't I freaking out?"

Fox sighed and headed downstairs to the kitchen to fix himself a bowl of cereal and sat at the island counter to eat it. He heard Cyanide in his ear, growling. Before he could ask the creature what was wrong, the front door opened.

"Fox? You up?" Samantha's voice called out.

"I'm up! In the kitchen!"

Cyanide's growls did not quiet down. If anything they got louder as Samantha entered the room. Fox began to wonder what its problem was. He wanted to ask, but not with Samantha in the room. She didn't need to know that the spells worked.

"*We should not trust her,*" Cyanide growled.

Fox really wanted to ask, but remained silent for now. Samantha sat down at the island counter next to him with her own bowl of cereal.

"You're looking much better this morning! So I guess it didn't work, huh? The spells, I mean," she said with a smile.

Fox shrugged, not wanting to mention it worked. "I guess not. Then again were we really expecting them to?"

"I suppose not. I'm glad though, I was ready to haul your ass off to the hospital," Samantha said with a smirk. "Finish your breakfast."

"Okay Mom," Fox said with a light tone. "I need to head back to my foster place and pack up after this. I want to get as much of my stuff moved over as I can before I officially claim it. It'll make things easier, especially since I've been here the last few nights."

"Just be careful, yeah?" Samantha said with worry in her voice.

"I will. He scares me but I'll be okay."

Samantha only nodded and the two finished their breakfast in an uncomfortable and tense silence. Fox was wondering why Cyanide was still growling at Samantha and why they shouldn't trust her.

Once breakfast was finished the two cleaned up the kitchen and Fox headed upstairs to his mother's bedroom to grab his phone then went to the office where he nabbed his bag then went back downstairs and found Samantha waiting by the door.

"Ready?" she asked.

"As I'll ever be," Fox muttered, softly with a hint of fear.

"I can give you a ride if you want."

"Nah. I'm in no hurry to get back, so I'll stick to walking. You should be careful driving back, okay? It's supposed to storm soon." Fox looked out the window by the door. "And judging by those clouds it's going to be a downpour any time now."

"That's why I offered a ride. I don't want you to get sick or your sketch pads to get wet," Samantha said.

"My sketch pads and tools are all upstairs in the office. They'll be safe here," Fox smiled.

She shrugged, " If you're sure. I'll see ya later then."

"I'll see ya Monday," he said.

Samantha gave him a hug and got into her car. She waved to Fox driving away.

Fox took in a deep breath, locked the house, and headed for home. He really didn't want to go back, but he needed to start packing his stuff so he could move in right after his birthday. He looked to the sky as he heard thunder rolling behind him. He started to walk a little faster but still in no hurry to return to his foster home.

"Hey, Cyanide?" Fox asked.

"*Yes?*" the creature growled.

"Why shouldn't we trust Samantha?"

"*I smelled blood on her hands,*" Cyanide said.

"Blood? Has she killed before? Or maybe someone she knew was killed," Fox asked a bit freaked out.

"*She has killed. Her hands are stained.*"

"How can you tell?"

"*You created me. Shouldn't you know?*"

Fox blushed. "Smartass."

A tense silence filled the air for a brief moment before Fox asked the real question that was bothering him.

"So we really can't trust her."

"*No,*" Cyanide growled.

"So much for having a friend." Fox sighed sadly.

"*Am I not a friend?*"

"No. I've been drawing you since I was nine. You're like a scary older brother," Fox said with a smile.

Cyanide growled softly, almost purring with content. *"If you say so."*

Fox chuckled, then groaned when he heard bikes approaching with two very grating voices calling to him.

"Hey, kitty cat!" Alex called.

"Fuck, not now," Fox groaned.

"Who are they?" Cyanide growled.

"No one, they're no one." Fox really didn't want to be on this subject.

"Hey! We're talking to you!" Baxter shouted.

Fox just kept on walking, not wanting to deal with those two, especially before having to deal with Mike. He stopped when Alex swerved his bike in front of him.

"Hey Dipshit, we're talking to you! What are you, deaf?" Alex said.

Fox growled under breath hearing Cyanide growl as well. Baxter came up from behind to corner Fox, and the two boys began their assault.

Cyanide was ready to come out when Fox commanded him otherwise. Fox didn't and hadn't fought back. If he did and went to prison he would lose his house and inheritance money. So he silently took the beating and held back Cyanide the best he could.

"Let me help you! I'll teach these pathetic little bitches a lesson!" Cyanide snarled.

'No! They might be garbage humans but we can't hurt them or kill them!' Fox said in his head to Cyanide.

BANG! A loud crack filled the air and the boys beating on Fox looked over to where the noise came from. A little old lady stood holding a shotgun. Fox smiled. He knew this angel in disguise.

"You hooligans, let my Fox go or I'll fill your asses with lead!" Doris growled at the boys.

Alex and Baxter were smart enough to realize the threat was real and booked it out of there. Fox slowly got up and headed over to Doris.

He gave her a bloody smile, "Aloha Doris, thanks for the save."

"Damn kids. This is why I spanked my young'uns. Taught them respect and kept them out of prison, then some damn hippies came in and said spanking was abuse. If that ain't a crock of shit," she said.

"Doris, you beat all," Fox said.

"Damn straight. Now come on darlin'. Let's get you cleaned up," Doris said with a motherly smile.

Fox followed Doris into her home and noticed some of her stuff was gone.

"Hey Doris, you moving or something?"

"No dear. Just putting some stuff in storage. Since George died I don't need a lot, but I've been putting it off for a while now. Figured it was time," she waved it off.

Fox nodded and headed into the kitchen with the elder woman. She had told him about George before, but not much. The man died about five years ago from lung cancer. No surprise as during his and Doris' time, smoking was more common. The thunder was louder and closer now.

Doris looks out the window, seeing the palm trees sway vigorously. "The storm is here but no rain yet."

Fox watched the trees while Doris patched him up. Lightning flashed brightly as thunder rattled the old home. Fox shivered, and then remembered something.

"Hey, Doris?"

"Yes, dear?"

"Where are your chickens?" Fox hadn't seen or heard them anywhere.

"They've gone to a new safe and happy home. Over the weekend I decided it was time to say goodbye to them," Doris said sadly.

Fox figured. He liked those chickens, they were pretty chill. The way Doris was talking was bothering him. It was like she was trying to say goodbye herself but more subtly.

Fox didn't mask his concern. "Doris, are you okay?"

"I'm fine, why?"

"Just making sure."

Doris winked at him. "That's why you're my favorite."

"Of course I am," Fox said with a smirk.

Doris scoffed playfully at that and finished patching him up.

"All set to go, sweet pea." Doris checked him over one last time.

"Mahalo," Fox said softly.

"What's wrong? Don't you dare tell me it's nothing," she said, using her motherly tone.

"It's just...I want to start packing up my things tonight so I can get to work on moving into the home my mother left, but that means facing him," he said with a shiver.

"Your bastard of a foster father," she growled.

Fox nodded and prayed Mike wasn't home when Doris came for him, but knew he didn't have that kind of luck. He spotted the familiar and hated truck in the drive when he followed her inside.

"You could always stay until he leaves in the morning for work," she said, pleading.

"Mahalo Doris, but I have to face the music sometime," Fox said sadly, but with a warm smile.

She sighed upset and palmed Fox's cheek gently like a mother comforting a child. "You come out alive, you hear me? You come out of that house alive. I don't care what happens to that bastard, but you better promise you'll be all right."

"I promise," Fox leaned into her touch.

"Just remember that once upon a time I practiced magic. Don't make me put an old Hawaiian curse on you," Doris joked through tears.

Fox laughed and hugged the elderly woman. He grabbed his bag and headed across the street. He turned to see Doris watching him closely through the window. He smiled sadly and headed inside.

Episode 10

Fox tiptoed into the house and tried to quietly make his way upstairs, but was caught. He flinched when he heard that dreaded voice calling him.

"Fox! Where the fuck have you been boy?"

"Like you care!" he shouted back.

"Don't you talk back to me!" Mike yelled, getting close to screaming as he stormed into the front hall.

"I wasn't talking back. This is talking back. I was telling the truth."

"Your mouth is going to get you killed, boy," his foster father snarled.

"You think so? I think it'll be my saving grace," Fox said with a smirk.

"Fucking smartass. We need to chat so shut up and listen," he growled.

Fox stared at Mike. He motioned for him to speak.

"You're turning eighteen soon," Mike said.

"Brilliant deduction Mike. What gave that away?"

"Cut the attitude before I beat it out of ya!" Mike threatened.

Fox rolled his eyes and motioned for him to continue once more, but didn't promise to hold his tongue.

"You know what happens when you turn eighteen?" Mike asked with a growl.

"I can finally get away from you," Fox said.

"Boy, you are pissing me off! Just shut the fuck up and listen!"

Fox crossed his arms and showed Mike he's not afraid. He knew it got under Mike's skin but he couldn't care less at this point. He just wanted to pack up and get the hell out of there.

"When you turn eighteen, you leave. When you leave the check I get from the state leaves with you."

"So?"

"So, I can't let that happen. You're not leaving," Mike said darkly.

"The fuck I'm not!"

"You belong to me boy! You hear!? You ain't leaving!" Mike yelled in a red hot rage.

Fox bolted up the stairs, not making it halfway before being grabbed from behind by his backpack, which was torn off of him and both were thrown down the stairs. Fox groaned and got up slowly but was knocked back down when Mike punched him in the face. He got up again and managed to evade Mike when he lunged at him. Mike crashed into the kitchen table with a loud CRACK! Seeing the man stunned and laying on the broken table, Fox took his chance and ran up the stairs.

He made it to his sisters' door and sensed something off. He opened the door and found something he never thought he'd see. Mike never touched Alice; he'd verbally abused her, but never hit her.

"Alice?" Fox asked, his voice a near whisper and shaking with horror.

Alice was covered in blood. She was battered and bruised, but the worst was that she was sliced up. Mike killed his own daughter.

"No. Oh, Alice," Fox said through tears. He clenched his eyes shut trying not to let the tears fall, but failed. "I'm so sorry, Alice. I should've been here."

He choked, fighting back sobs. He couldn't hold it in. He cried. After a moment he let out a scream of pain and anger. His skin was turning black and melting off to reveal bones.

"Little bastard! You want to fight? Get back here and fight me like a man!" Mike screamed.

Fox snarled viciously. His left hand was now a large skeletal wolf's paw. He heard Mike coming up the stairs and stopped at the door.

"Ah. Little bitch decided to defend you and wouldn't back down. I finally got annoyed with her and her shit so I sent her to be with her mother. They can rot in Hell together," Mike said with a mix of pride, triumph, and annoyance.

"It's not Hell they'll be going to," Fox and Cyanide said in unison.

Mike looked at Fox scared, confused, but mostly with rage, "Fucking punk!"

Fox/Cyanide laughed together like a madman. Fox/Cyanide turned around and looked at Mike, gaining satisfaction to see the man looking so scared of him. One half of his face was melted off revealing his skull underneath, his skin was black and ink-like, and was melting off the rest of him. He seemed more wolf-like than human.

"The fuck are you?" Mike asked fearfully.

Fox/Cyanide took his skeletal wolf paw and stabbed Mike. He yanked his claws free of the now-dead bastard then flicked away the heart that he managed to take out. He turned to Alice once more as he started to return to normal. He sighed sadly as he believed if he were here, he could've saved her or at least tried.

"She'd still be alive if it weren't for me," Fox said tearfully.

Cyanide said nothing. Not even a growl. In the comics, Cyanide didn't have much empathy, but then again in the comics, he was not fused to a human.

Fox went to say something more when he heard a sound. It was Cyanide growling.

"What's up?" Fox asked.

Before anyone said anything, Fox heard a loud CRASH! The window shattered. He felt a white-hot pain in his stomach and his shirt was getting wet. He looked down and saw blood blossoming out across the cloth. With a shaky hand, he lifted up the fabric to reveal a bullet wound.

"F-fuck...need m-my phone..." Fox panted.

Fox painstakingly made his way to the stairs where he actually debated with himself and Cyanide if he could make it.

"Fuck...I-I can't..." he gasped.

"You're going to have to if you don't want to die!" Cyanide growled.

"W-why can't w-we j-just transform?" Fox panted in pain.

"I could cause more damage to the wound. Just go slow."

Fox did exactly as Cyanide said. He slowly made his way down until a wave of dizziness hit him and he fell down the last three steps. He screamed in pain and let loose a few tears.

Fox managed to open his eyes once more and spotted his backpack where it landed during the fight. The object got thrown to the right of him where the front hall was. He gathered just enough strength to army crawl toward it. When he got close enough he opened the bag and felt around for his phone. He pulled it out and dialed 9-1-1 and tried to speak.

"9-1-1, what's your emergency?" the male dispatcher asked.

"H-help me," Fox pleaded weakly, fading fast.

"What's the problem, sir?" the dispatcher asked calmly.

"I-I was s-shot...my s-sister...k-killed...p-please...h -help..." Fox gasped out.

"I've got your location and police and EMTs are on their way. I want you to try and stay awake for me, all right? What's your name?" the dispatcher replied.

"F-fox...h-hurts...p-please..."

"Hold on for me Fox. Don't you dare pass out on me!" the dispatcher exclaimed.

"S-so...c-cold..." Fox whispered.

If the man said something, Fox didn't hear it. Everything sounded as though it was underwater. His vision wasn't blurry anymore, but near black. He couldn't breathe. He was cold and sleepy. He could faintly hear Cyanide barking at him. He closed his eyes and let the darkness take him under into sweet oblivion.

Episode 11

Fox floated peacefully on a still lake on his back. No winds to flip him into the water beneath him, just the warm sun beaming down on his skin. It was quiet. No birds around to chirp and the trees did not sway. Just silence.

The only thing there was Cyanide. The ink being was lying in the grass like a normal wolf and even seemed like a normal wolf. Its ink was like fur and covered half of its body. It seemed so real and normal. The beast kept a watchful eye on Fox.

"Fox?" Cyanide asked.

"Yeah, Cyanide?"

"I believe it is time for you to wake up," the creature said.

"Why? Maybe it's my time."

"Fox-" Cyanide began.

"Don't. This isn't some 'I'm giving up because there's nothing left' speech. I've been alone all my life. I'm used to it. I'm just saying, maybe it's my time now. I've tried waking up, you know," Fox pointed at the creature then laid his arm back in the water.

Cyanide sat up and glared at Fox. "Not hard enough. We have work to do, now get out of the water, stop pouting and wake up."

"What work?" Fox giving Cyanide a pointed look.

"The one that injured you. They have familiar blood," Cyanide growled.

"Familiar blood? The hell does that mean?" Fox demanded in confusion.

"It means they have some relation to you."

"Relation?" A thought hits Fox like a ton of bricks. "Sonovabitch."

Cyanide watched as Fox got out of the water and paced back and forth on the ground before him. It didn't say anything but watched, silently hoping that Fox would calm down enough to tell it what was going on in his mind.

"Samantha. She found this police report from the night my parents died. I thought for sure it was a fake, just something to screw with me. I'm not so sure now," Fox explained.

"What does this report say?" The beast asked, tilting his head to the side.

"That my father's body went missing the night he and my mom died," Fox said. He stopped pacing and was now biting his knuckle.

"Your father must be alive then, and it's his blood I smelled," Cyanide said.

"Fuck my life. Just fuck it sideways to Sunday!" Fox exclaimed angrily.

Fox began to pace once more. He took his knuckle out of his mouth and gripped his hair, muttering as he walked back and forth.

"Wait? How the hell did he get into my house!? It has protection sigils on the door."

"Sigils can be altered and manipulated," Cyanide stated.

"True. Very true. So what now? How do I wake up?" Fox asked, finally getting with it.

"Believe in your strengths," Cyanide said.

Fox looked over at Cyanide and tilted his head to the side.

"Did you just quote Legend of Zelda?" Fox asked, surprised while holding back a smile and a laugh.

"Legend of whom now?" Cyanide asked.

"Right. Scary ink monster," Fox muttered, then nodded and clapped his hands together. "All right, believe in my strengths."

Fox closed his eyes to think of ways of getting out of here and came up with nothing.

"GAH! Stupid! Useless empty brain! It's like having writers' block but I'm not writing anything! Pfft."

Fox plopped onto the ground and stared at the cloudless sky once more. He closed his eyes and started to think of his mother. He didn't remember much of her now. He should feel bad about that but he didn't. He barely even knew his mother, and now with all this coming to light, how his comics are actually based on real things and not a child's fever dream, he began to wonder if this was real life or if he was actually dead. Death would explain why he wasn't freaking out and still a wee bit sane. Fox began to drift without realizing it but didn't fall asleep completely.

Cyanide watched over the dozing boy. It knew he'd wake up soon.

Fox bolted up with an idea.

"I got it! I know how to wake up!"

Cyanide growled lowly in response and watched the boy stand up in excitement.

Fox stood and closed his eyes in concentration. He pictured his mother and her voice. He imagined what she would tell him if she were still alive.

"That's it, Fox. Come on Kit, you can do it. Let me see those beautiful eyes," his mother said encouragingly.

Fox focused on that one little thing until he felt himself waking up.

Episode 12

Fox opened his eyes to harsh light. He flinched and closed them. He heard a voice but didn't recognize it.

"Sorry about that, sweetie. Let's dim those lights for you."

She dimmed the lights, and when he opened his eyes again he saw a doctor coming in, chart clutched in one hand.

She smiled at Fox. "Good to see you awake, Mr. Kane. I'm Dr. Katrina Alaverez."

"How long-?" Fox rasped, wincing at the pain from his throat.

"Two weeks. Your wounds were pretty serious. We were mostly worried about the gunshot wound, but we fixed it up. You'll be good as new in no time. Luckily for you the bullet went straight through and missed everything vital. The reason we were worried about it was because of the blood loss. The other wounds, however, really worry me. Be honest with me Fox, were you abused?" she asked.

"Yes. My last foster father, Mike, was pretty abusive," Fox said hesitantly.

"I see. I don't know if you remember, but you and your foster family were attacked. You were the only survivor, I'm afraid, although since you were being abused I can't say I'm sorry to see an abuser six feet under," Katrina said.

Fox didn't say anything as he remembered everything. He was the one that killed that asshole. He was finally free of that man. He mustered up some fake tears and let them fall.

"My foster sister. She took good care of me. She didn't survive?" Fox asked, playing dumb.

The doctor looked at Fox sadly. "I'm so sorry love, but no. Her injuries were not only severe but she was already gone by the time EMTs arrived at the house. She's at peace now, though." She gently pat his blanket-clad leg.

Fox nodded, his tears real this time. He wiped his face and looked at the doctor once more.

"What'll happen to me now?" he asked, knowing what'll happen.

"A social worker is here about that, but they're not to see you yet. I want you to rest, you just woke up and I'd hate for you to relapse," Katrina said.

Fox nodded and let the doctor and nurse look him over and check his wounds. He drifted off to sleep after feeling a warm tingling sensation. He didn't dream this time around, and that was probably due to Cyanide. He was thankful either way, sometimes all you need is blissful darkness.

Two days later, the doctor let the social worker talk to him.

"Hello, Mr. Kane. I'm Keith Manning and I need to talk to you about your future," the man said.

"I know why you're here," Fox said as a matter-of-factly and a little smug.

"Well, then. Let's begin. I know there's a will-" Keith started before Fox interrupted.

"The will my mother left I know of it and I have the original. It states that all her assets and the estate are mine. I've turned eighteen; it would be pointless to put me with another family. In fact, you can't," Fox said with a smirk. He had turned eighteen while in his coma. "I checked my mothers' accounts and found she has quite the fortune. I'm set for life. So, here's my future. Once I get out of this hospital, I'll go back to my last foster home and pack up what's left, then I'll move into my Mom's house."

The social worker stared at Fox as if he admitted something horrible and finally said something.

"Y-you're eighteen?" he asked.

Fox simply nodded, the smirk still upon his face.

"W-well I need proof! Otherwise, you're a minor!" Keith exclaimed.

Fox sighed and showed the caseworker his bracelet. Hospital bracelets always have your date of birth on them. Fox one, caseworker zero.

"I-I-" Keith stammered.

"Dude, give it up. I'm eighteen and there's nothing you can do. I'm going to be graduating high school here in a few weeks and I have a small fortune to keep me going for years, so no worries on money," Fox said with a yawn.

Keith was about to say something when his doctor came in and dismissed the social worker saying his time was up and her patient needed rest.

"We'll be in touch, Mr. Kane," Keith swore.

Fox rolled his eyes and waved at the man.

Katrina came back in to check him over. He sat still long enough for her to do the exam and then started joking.

"Give it to me straight doc, am I ever going to play the piano again?" Fox asked.

"Good to see a sense of humor. Usually, my patients are whining for more drugs. As far as the piano you strike me more of a drum man," Katrina snorted.

"Ha! I have to admit drum guys don't get a lot of love. It's mostly the singer and guitar guys," Fox said with a chuckle.

"That's because they sell their souls to the devil. The drum guys are at least honest and the bands wouldn't be anything without them."

"True. True."

There was an air of silence for a brief moment.

"How'd it go?" Katrina asked.

Fox scoffed, "As you'd expect. No disrespect or anything, Doc, but all I want to do is get out of here and move into my mom's house."

"No disrespect or anything was taken. You're not my first foster kid. Sadly, I've taken care of many other foster kids way before you were even a thought," she said.

"Were they all abused, too?" Fox asked.

"As much as it pains me to say, a good chunk of them were. The others were in good homes though," Katrina said softly.

He nodded sadly, "Yeah, good homes these days are becoming harder to find. It's easy to hide abuse if you know how."

"'Tis very sad, indeed. One day abusers of all kinds will reap what they sow," Katrina said with hope.

"I wish," Fox said softly looking down at his blanket-clad legs.

"They will. All right, get some rest and I'll be back later," Katrina said.

"Okay. When will I be discharged?"

"Let's see what tomorrow brings, yeah?" Katrina asked with a chuckle.

Fox nodded and laid back against the pillows as the good doctor left. He had hoped to be out of there by tonight so as to avoid the social worker again, but looked like he would be staying the rest of that day. He laid back and watched TV well into the night.

He dozed off at some point and woke up early. He was determined that today he was being released, even if he had to check out AMA.

Katrina walked in with a stack of papers and a small white bag with something folded neatly in her arms.

"I come bearing gifts," she said with a smile.

"Oh?" Fox asked.

"Since you're doing so well and healing nicely from your wounds, I decided if you go easy for a bit and get help moving into your mother's home, then you can leave. I brought some clothes for you to wear, well scrubs really, but it's better than going in your underwear. I also have the antibiotics that you need to continue to take. While you were in a coma, you had a fever due to an infection which is going away, thankfully. The painkillers you should take for at least the first week but the antibiotic I want you to finish no matter how good you feel, hear me?" Katrina asked, giving Fox a pointed look.

Fox excitedly said. "Doc, you're awesome! Where do I sign?"

Katrina chuckled. "Calm down. Just sign on these two pages," she pointed to the papers. "Then you can go shower, just be careful and you can dress in these scrubs. We had to cut off your clothes, but your shoes are still intact and in the cabinet there." She pointed to the cabinet in the corner of the room.

Fox nodded and signed the papers. While he signed, the doctor checked his vitals and wounds one more time and then took his IV out. He handed her the papers when he was finished. Being careful, Fox showered and dressed in the scrubs the doctor brought him. He put his shoes on and pocketed the medicines and then thanked the doctor for everything.

"It's my job after all. Just get going before that social worker comes back," Katrina said.

"He can't do anything anyway. I'm eighteen now," Fox said with a smug smile.

"No, he can't. Legally anyway. He will try the lawyer card and find some way around it to get his way," Katrina said. "Now go. Just be sure to take care of that wound."

Fox nodded and thanked her again. He headed down the corridor to the elevator. When he reached the main lobby, he carefully made his way to the door while trying to blend in.

Fox spotted his social worker talking on his cell phone in the corner of the room. He panicked for a second and hid in the bathroom back down the hallway. He sighed when he saw there was no one else inside but him. He hid in the handicap stall and brought his knuckle up to his mouth and nibbled on it.

"Fuck me, he's here already. What should I do?" Fox muttered.

"I have an idea. I can make you into a shadow; all you have to do is stick to the shadows out there. No one will see us," Cyanide rumbled.

"Better than nothing I suppose," Fox said with a shrug.

Cyanide growled lowly in agreement and Fox nodded then concentrated. He watched as the ink flowed inside of him and turned him completely black. Then he stepped out of the stall and blended into the shadows.

He made his way out of the hospital without being seen and continued to blend into the shadows as he made his way back to his last foster home.

Episode 13

He made his way in and changed back to normal. Before going inside, he noticed that Doris' place was dark. He decided to go over real quick and see what was up.

Fox looked into the window and found the living room totally empty, as if no one had ever lived there. He went around to the back and slipped in through the sliding door. The lock mechanism was broken and Doris never bothered getting it fixed. Fox looked around the kitchen and it, too, was empty.

"Doris?" he called out.

No answer. He called again. Nothing. He looked around the one-story home and still nothing. Doris was gone. He should be mad, but he wasn't. He kinda figured she had lied to him. He sighed sadly and hoped she was alright wherever she was now. He left the home and headed back over to the hell hole that was his foster home.

He looked back at Doris' home. "Mahalo Doris, for everything. A hui hou."

He went back across the street to do what he came to do. Fox packed up what little possessions and clothes he had into the boxes he'd saved while he bounced around, then sealed them up. He took them downstairs carefully one by one, even though there were only three he didn't want to wind up back in the hospital.

Fox considered taking the truck, but he didn't trust it. He then remembered there was a four-wheeler that Mike kept gassed up in the garage.

He went to the garage and saw the four-wheeler. He praised whatever deity is in the sky for it having the key in the ignition. Fox placed the boxes on the back of the vehicle and made sure they were secure. He went back in and grabbed his backpack and duffel bag, then got on the four-wheeler.

Fox didn't worry about getting caught as people rode ATVs and go-karts up and down the streets all the time. Plus, he was only going ten minutes away. He started the thing up and headed for home. He parked the vehicle in the garage he hadn't been in yet.

"Dayum. If I had known there was a '67 Impala in here, I would've been ridin' in style," Fox said with a whistle.

After admiring his new car, he brought his stuff inside slowly one by one as he did at Mikes. By the time he brought his last box in, he was tired and hurting. He set the box down in the den with the others and took in a shaking deep breath.

Fox decided it was time for lunch and a nap. He grabbed his meds and cooked himself some ramen noodles Samantha had brought for him.

"I know I shouldn't trust this but my medicine says to take with food and I'm too tired to head back out," Fox said to himself.

Cyanide growled, not liking the idea of Fox eating something from that woman.

"I know bud, but if I take it without food I could get sick. I'd rather risk it than spend the night awake in pain."

Cyanide huffed in reluctant agreement. It didn't want Fox to get sick; the boy was just beginning to heal. The creature wished it could heal Fox but it didn't have healing abilities. Fox never gave the being any, in the comics. Now that he was real, it wasn't sure. Cyanide was created as a natural speed healer if it got hurt, although if it was in a pinch and needed healing fast, it could always use its ink to heal. The problem with that is that it took a lot of energy that the creature would need in battle.

Theoretically, Cyanide could heal Fox or Fox could heal himself with the ink, but it would take the energy they both need, and right now Fox needed all he could get.

After Fox finished his lunch and took his medicine. He looked at the winding staircase at the end of the hallway and snorted.

"Don't think I can make it upstairs right now. The couch sounds like a death sentence but it'll do for now," he muttered tiredly.

Fox made his way to the living room and settled on the long furniture. He pulled the afghan from the back and snuggled underneath it. He let the medicine wash over him, and he fell into blissful darkness.

Elsewhere-The Warehouse District

A black SUV pulled into the warehouse district. Two people got out of the vehicle and walked up to a warehouse. The man unlocked the door and opened it, allowing the woman to walk in. The warehouse reeked of dead fish and salt. The waves outside crashed against the docks and made an echo inside. Most of the metal of the old building was rusted and weathered. It was falling apart, but would have to do for now.

Samantha entered the warehouse and wrinkled her nose at the smell. Warehouses gave her the creeps.

"A bit cliché don't you think mate?" she asked with a snarl.

"It's the best we can do for now, plus this place is close to my girl's old place."

Samantha looked at him, surprised, "Really? So we're near Fox? How far away?"

"Like, fifteen minutes out."

"Geez," she scoffed.

"Islands. Everything's close and within walking distance," Maddox pointed out.

"True. All right, so how are we playing this?" Samantha asked, crossing her arms over her chest.

"You're going to gain his trust back, because I know that creature has probably already filled his head with lies and Fox won't trust you."

"Right. So I gain his trust back and lure him here. How?"

"A fake kidnapping, of course," Maddox said all too casually.

"Will that even work? This creature is probably smart." Samantha raised her eyebrows.

"Oh it's smart, but it's not the creature we're trying to lure."

Samantha nodded. There was one more question on her mind that she needed to be sure of.

"Are you sure, and I mean absolutely sure, that Fox is even alive? Last I heard he was circling the drain."

"I'm positive. I went to the hospital he was taken to. He was in a coma for two weeks and then discharged this morning," Maddox said with certainty.

"What about the blood? Is his blood even blood?"

"He's able to disguise his blood as ink and vice versa. I can't really explain it," Maddox said unsure. "At least I think he can."

"Maybe being bound to the creature naturally turned his blood," Samantha theorized. "Interesting. Important question. When?"

"After your graduation. So, the Monday after," Maddox said.

Samantha nodded and left. She had some planning of her own to do. From what little time she had spent with Fox, she knew he was strong-minded. He wouldn't be easy to sway, but she had to. This was her mission, not his.

'The last of her organization will finally be extinct. Revenge is a dish best served cold after all,' she snarled in her thoughts.

Episode 14

Today was a big day. Graduation day. A month ago he was in a coma and moved into his mother's home and now, he was walking the stage. He looked heavenward.

"I did it, Mom. I'm graduating," Fox whispered to the ceiling.

Fox stood in the dressing room at the performance hall where his graduation was being held. He was dressed in black dress pants and a deep forest green button-down shirt. His usually-spiked hair was combed neatly. He cleaned up nicely. The boys had black robes and caps while the girls had navy blue. Fox zipped up his robe and looked in the mirror.

"This robe makes me look like a goober," he muttered.

"Well, I think you look handsome," a voice behind him said.

Fox looked over at Samantha and wanted to bolt. He was a little surprised that Cyanide wasn't growling or snarling.

"*She's up to something. Just play along for the time being,*" Cyanide said calmly.

"Fox, I owe you an apology," Samantha said, softly and sadly.

"What for? What did you do wrong?" he asked, playing along.

"I wasn't there for you when you got hurt. I just sort of vanished. A good mate is always there."

Fox looked at Samantha and inwardly sighed as Cyanide huffed.

"I forgive you, though I was sleeping half the time and would've barely remembered if you were there," he lied through his teeth.

Samantha hugged Fox gently, not sure if he was still hurt or hurting. She let go and looked at him, and then fussed with his robe and cap, making sure the tassel was on the right side. The two looked at the TV screen when it came to life.

"Attention students and families. We are ready to begin the ceremony. Families, please take your seats and students please head backstage," the principal announced.

The TV flickered to the screensaver it had been on and the two headed for the stage. Fox sat in his seat. Despite everything, he was valedictorian. He knew if his mother were alive she would be very proud of him.

Fox watched the ceremony go on with everyone getting their diplomas. He retrieved his diploma when his name was called and returned to his place on stage. Soon came time for his speech.

"Now our valedictorian, Fox Kane!" the principal announced proudly.

Polite applause sounded as Fox stood up and walked to the podium to deliver the speech he made up on the fly, because he had been busy with other things. When the clapping stopped, he began.

"Class of twenty nineteen. What a year it has been. We've all had our ups and downs, some more than others, but what makes me happy is that we never gave up. We kept fighting until we saw on our calendars that we would soon be free from the shackles of high school!" Fox said and laughed with the audience. "However, the journey of life is far from over. We must now venture out and tackle life. Some of us plan to go to college while the rest of us aren't sure what is in store for us and that's okay! It's okay not to know. So stumble, fall, eat dirt, get back up, and just keep fighting. You'll find your answer. Follow your heart, chase your dreams, and more importantly get a little messy. Life's messy, so why not? Congrats class of twenty nineteen! Good luck in the real world!"

The audience and students clapped and cheered. Then turned their tassels and tossed their caps into the air, then turned to hug fellow classmates.

Episode 15

Later that evening Fox was in the living room sketching his latest comic strip, as a nagging thought he fought to keep away all day came back to him full force.

"Hey, Cyanide?" Fox asked.

Cyanide hummed in response. Fox thought that was strange as it usually growled, but shrugged it off.

"What did you mean that Samantha was up to something?" Fox asked curiously. The thought had been bugging him since the ceremony.

"I smelled ill intent on her. She plans to do something to you, to us. I am willing to bet she is working with the one who smells of familiar blood," Cyanide rumbled.

Fox didn't want to believe it at first, but with all that'd happened within the last few weeks, he was honestly not surprised. Though, he wished he knew the real reason why Samantha was doing this. He also needed to know if this person of familiar blood was really his father.

"Well, that's just fan-fucking-tastic. My dead father is possibly alive and hunting me for reasons I don't fucking know, and Samantha is actually his bitch, trailing after him like a little lost puppy for again some shitty reason I don't know! GAH! This is balls-up-the-wall insane and I'm probably going mad!" Fox shouted in frustration. His life was getting a bit crazy, like some characters in your favorite superhero comic book.

"Calm yourself, Fox. Getting worked up will solve nothing!"

Fox threw his arms up in the air and shouted, "I can't freaking help it! All of this is like some whacked-out fever dream that I can't wake up from! For fuck's sake, I should be freaking out since I'm fused to an ink monster!"

"Calm down now!" Cyanide barked loudly and menacingly.

Fox stilled and quieted his mind. Cyanide was scary as hell when it was angry. Even in his comics it was menacing when it was mad.

"Good. Now then. The only thing we can do for the time being is lay low and plan," Cyanide rumbled.

"Do you know what she and my possibly-alive father are planning?" Fox asked.

"No. What I do know is that they are going to take you and me down, or at least try," Cyanide said.

"Like in my comic! The leader of The Underground wanted to take you out but he couldn't. You managed to slip away," Fox supplied the obvious. Thanks, captain.

"Yes, I remember. I also remember he had a partner. I slaughtered them I believe." Cyanide almost purred in happiness.

"You did. Quite brutally..." Fox trailed off as a thought slammed into him like a drunk driver. "Sonovabitch."

Cyanide growled in question.

"My father killed my mother," Fox said, his eyes blank and his voice void of any emotions.

"How do you know?" Cyanide asked.

"I had a dream a while ago. It was a dream I've had for years after my parents died. It faded into the background but came around once and a while. I had it recently, well, before all this happened. I was six years old and it was thunder storming. I wanted my mother and went to look for her when she didn't answer me. I came down the stairs and went to the kitchen as I figured she'd be outside watching the storm on the beach. I looked out the back doors and saw a skeletal wolf-like creature in the lightning," Fox explained.

"*Like me,*" Cyanide rumbled.

"Give or take a few details, but yeah. I screamed and woke up. Thinking about it and putting together all the pieces of what's been happening lately, I don't think it's a dream. I think it's a memory, and if it's a memory then everything makes sense," Fox said, biting his knuckle. This whole thing was giving him a headache.

"*What makes sense?*" Cyanide asked, confused.

"The reason why my mother has an altar in a hidden room, and all the magic stuff. It makes all the sense. The picture on the cave wall at the cove Samantha and I visited, the Poison Lei picture, it's all real. My mother was part of an organization that uses magic to commit crimes. My comics aren't fiction," Fox said with an emotionless chuckle. "How many people can say that?"

"*So if your drawings are real, what plan do you have?*" Cyanide asked.

Fox sat back down on the couch and ran a hand down his face, "Not sure. My father's character disappears after you were wounded, well more like me, but you get the gist. He doesn't reappear until a year later. If he's here now, he's probably laying low and will send Samantha to do his dirty work."

"*So what do we do?*" Cyanide asked, needing to know.

"Like you said at the ceremony. We play along, then I kill my father," Fox said
nonchalantly.

"*For your mother?*" the creature rumbled softly.

"Yeah, among other things," Fox growled.

"*Among other things?*"

"He's trying to kill me, and would've killed me that night if my mother hadn't wounded him to the point of death. He wants me dead because of my mother, so I need to kill him before he gets to me."

"*So we just sit back and play along?*"

"You ask a lot of questions, pal," Fox joked.

Cyanide snarled and Fox barked a laugh.

"Anyway, yes. For now, we play along. As you said, Samantha's up to something and for the time being we lay low," Fox said, still smirking.

"*And our plan?*" Cyanide asked.

"We'll improvise," Fox said with a shrug.

Cyanide huffed a frustrated growl but said nothing more for the rest of the night. Fox was okay with it and went back to drawing. Despite everything, he wanted to continue Cyanides' story.

Fox finished the sketch and took it upstairs to the office where his other sketch pads and art supplies were. He grabbed the very first comic pages he drew of Cyanide and scanned them with the printer, then uploaded them to a file on his own laptop, which he set up the night after he moved in. He went over the pages and uploaded the file online.

"Let's see how the world likes a scary anti-hero," Fox said nervously, his heart racing.

Fox then made a Twitter page for his comic and promoted the first pages with a link to them. He closed his laptop and headed down the winding staircase to make some dinner. Fox's phone was in his bedroom ringing and he frowned when he heard the loud ringtone. No one had his new phone number.

He raced back up to see who would be calling. The phone stopped ringing before Fox got there, and he picked it up to check the caller ID when it rang once more. He hesitated, but answered anyway.

"Hello?"

"*Fox! Thank god. I've been taken; I was out to dinner with my father when my phone rang. I went outside to answer it and I got snatched!*" Samantha whispered on the other end.

Fox didn't buy it, but played along like he planned and said. "Do you know where you are?"

"*N-no,*" she cried, not knowing Fox could tell they were fake tears. "*But I heard them. We're going to the warehouse district.*"

"All right, try and call the police if you can. I'm on my way," Fox, with fake urgency, pretended to sound concerned.

"*Please, please hurry,*" she whispered.

"*Hey! What are you doing?*" a man in the background shouted.

"*No! Get back!*" she screamed.

Fox pulled the phone away from his ear, then hung up and made his way downstairs. He was not in any hurry as he knew it was a trap.

"*Are we going?*" Cyanide asked.

"Why not? It's a nice night, why not have a little fun?" Fox asked.

Since the warehouse district wasn't too far from his home, he decided it was a beautiful night for a stroll. He left the house and walked in the direction of the warehouses. He enjoyed his walk, letting the gentle ocean breeze cool him off. It was pretty hot despite the fact it was near ten at night.

As he walked, he let Cyanide slowly creep out. His black veins spread throughout his body as the ink flowed, but he didn't fully transform. He was halfway there but the full thing would come soon. The black veins were hidden as they got closer, and Fox's skin was the ashen grey it had been when he first performed the spells.

Fox smirked as Cyanide began to growl. They were almost there.

At Warehouse Number Nine

Activity was being set for the trap for Fox.

"Are you sure he's coming?" Maddox asked, while tying Samantha down to a chair to make the kidnapping seem real.

"Of course. He wouldn't leave me in this situation. Ouch! Not so tight asshole!" Samantha said with an eye roll.

"Right because you're such a convincing actress. The ropes wouldn't be so tight if you'd stop moving," Maddox snarked.

"For all I know you could've done it on purpose, and I think I did fan-bloody-tastic. I deserve an Oscar," Samantha bragged.

Maddox huffed and began to say, "What you deserve-"

Maddox was cut off by a loud SMASH! The two looked up to see the skylight had been broken, with a dark substance oozing off of it.

"What the fuck was that and what the hell is that dark shit?!" Maddox exclaimed.

"How the hell should I know!?" Samantha argued.

The two watched as the substance continued to drip. The warehouse was silent for a few moments before it was broken by a female voice.

"Well, don't just stand there like a bleeding idiot! Go see what it is!" Samantha commanded.

Maddox rolled his eyes and mumbled something under his breath, but listened. He went over to see what the substance was and found it was not blood, like he was thinking. He dipped his fingers in it and brought it up closer to his face for inspection. He found the black liquid smelled like a permanent marker.

"I think this is ink," Maddox said, and sniffed it again to be sure. "Yup. Smells like it. It also has that texture and feel."

"Ink? What the hell is ink doing here?" Samantha asked.

"Someone must be out there. I'm going to go look," Maddox said, and walked over to the table where his weapons were laid out. He chose a gun.

"Untie me first!" Samantha shouted.

"If it's my son, you'll be fine. Just stick to the plan," Maddox said, not too worried.

"What plan? We never discussed one!" Samantha yelled.

"You'll be fine. I'll be back."

Maddox left and Samantha threw her head back and groaned.

"Son of a bleeding bitch. That cock could've at least untied me," she muttered under her breath.

"That would've been no fun," Fox/Cyanide said from somewhere in the shadows.

"Fox!?" Samantha exclaimed.

She looked around and didn't see him anywhere.

"Fox, where are you? Why do you sound so weird?" Samantha asked, getting nervous.

"I'm right here," Fox/Cyanide said.

Samantha looked around again and still didn't see Fox anywhere.

She was about to call out to him again when she spotted something coming out of the ink puddle. It looked yellowish and bony. A large claw poked out of the ink and slowly the rest of the creature emerged from the puddle. When the creature fully emerged, the ink puddle ran up the wolf-like creature and covered half of it like a protective skin.

Samantha struggled for words. She remained silent for a moment before finally speaking.

"F-Fox?" she stuttered in a whisper.

The creature didn't move. Just stared.

"Fox, the spells...they actually worked?"

"They did," Fox/Cyanide rumbled, almost growling.

"What are you?" she whispered curiously and somewhat fearfully.

"A new kind of Cyanide. What are you?" the creature snarled.

"What do you mean?"

"You know what," Fox/Cyanide growled.

"I'm-" she began.

POP POP POP! Gunshots rang out, but didn't faze the creature as the shots somehow missed it.

"Is that any way of saying hello to your son after trying to kill him all those years ago?" Fox/Cyanide said with a sinister smirk.

"I couldn't let your mother poison your mind with this magic nonsense. Then when it turned out to be true and there really was an organization that used magic to commit their crimes, I had to stop her before she converted you. I see she sunk her claws into you anyhow," Maddox declared.

The creature laughed menacingly with a slight growl. "My mother poisoned me? That's a laugh!"

"She did! Look at you!" Maddox shouted.

"I barely know anything about her and why she chose the path she did, but I'm not following in her footsteps. I obey no one and I have no master," the creature snarled, and bared its terrifying teeth.

"If you're not following in her footsteps, why perform the spells!?" Maddox demanded.

"Curiosity. Simple as that," Fox/Cyanide said.

"That's bullshit!"

"Believe what you will, but I speak the truth," the beast rumbled.

"Fox was that you or Cyanide talking?" Samantha asked.

"Both of us. We are one," the ink beast said.

Fox came through. "But we can speak separately."

Cyanide came through. "We share the same body, not the mind or soul."

"Since you can talk separately, can you separate from each other in that form?" Samantha asked curiously.

Both Cyanide and Fox came through again "Why should we tell you?"

"We can help you! Fox, we can separate you and you'll have a normal life again," Samantha pleaded.

The beast laughed like a madman and Fox came through to speak.

"Why would I do that, and what normal life? I've been a foster kid that bounced from home to home. Some nice, while others were a living Hell. Why give this up? I feel free."

POP POP POP!

Maddox held his gun and was panting. The creature looked down at its bones and saw a bullet lodged in one of the ribs on the right side. The creature reached up with a claw and pulled it out.

"Was that supposed to hurt?" Fox/Cyanide asked.

Maddox was ready to shoot again when the creature allowed the ink to slip off to the floor and it vanished back into the puddle, jumping into the shadows of the warehouse.

"Fox!" Maddox yelled.

"Maddox, untie me!" Samantha demanded as she struggled in the ropes.

Maddox untied her and the two tried to escape. The creature jumped out with a menacing roar, blocking the door.

"Leaving so soon, Dad? I thought we'd sit down and talk some more," Fox said with a smirk that would make the bravest man scared.

"Son, come with me. We'll get you cured and you can join me! My organization hunts down The Poison Lei cultists and puts an end to them and their ways. If you come with me, we can make you an agent," Maddox pleaded.

"Cure me?" Fox asked.

"There is no cure," Cyanide growled.

"Even if there was, there's a tiny little problem," Fox said.

Samantha spoke up. "Fox, think about it! You can be with us and I won't have to get my revenge," she said, trying to make Fox and not the beast to see reason.

The beast turned its horrifying gaze onto Samantha, and she flinched. She didn't want to do this, but she wanted all this madness to end.

"This is just a revenge story for you?" Fox snarled.

"My parents were tortured and killed by these bastards after "betraying" them! You can't blame me here!"

"Were your parents a part of the cult?" Fox tilted his head.

"Yeah. One of the rules is that you can't have children. Rules were made to be broken, I suppose," Samantha spat.

"If that's true, how are we still alive?" Fox asked.

"I'm alive because I'm fucking protecting the world from monsters like you! You'll die, though. I'll see to it. This is my operation, not your father's," Samantha exclaimed angrily.

Maddox was about to say something when he was cut off.

"A monster, am I?" Fox gave a gruesome smirk.

"No. Not yet. You know, I don't have to kill you. We can help you, and cure you. Just come with us. Please. I don't want to hurt you."

Fox was silent once more, before laughing. "Like I was saying before. There's a tiny little problem."

"What's that? Tell me you didn't perform a spell that leaves you like this forever!" Samantha now begged.

"No. We like the disease!" Fox/Cyanide howled menacingly.

Fox lunged at them, pinned Samantha to the floor, and took a chunk out of her shoulder. It listened to her scream bloody murder, when Maddox fired the gun again. The creature jumped off of her and felt a few bullets hit its front legs and collarbone.

"Ouch. That hurt," Fox/Cyanide said, both voices dripping sarcasm.

The creature disappeared into the shadows, only to reappear behind his father. It swiped a massive claw at him, throwing Maddox halfway across the room. Maddox slammed into some crates and rolled to a stop. The creature noticed Samantha army crawling across the floor to get to the exit. He pinned her to the ground once more and looked at her, seeing the fear etched on her face.

"I should spare you, but like those bullies, you'll just keep coming back until your clichéd revenge story is complete," Fox snarled.

"Fo-ox...ple-please...I didn't w-want this...all I-I want-ted-" Samantha gasped in pain.

"Let me guess, avenge your beloved fallen parents? HAHAHA! So you came after me thinking it would ease your pain. News flash, it wouldn't."

"Y-your m-mother was the o-ne who did i-it...D-daddy over there w-wanted t-to kill y-you first..." Samantha painfully rasped.

"Doesn't surprise me. And how do you know? If my father told you, he could've lied to you. Lied to get to me. Ever think about that?" Fox growled.

Samantha didn't answer, just coughed up more blood and took in a shaky breath.

"I trusted you when every fucking fiber of my being said not to. Rule one being a foster kid, trust no one and make no connections," Fox snarled. Trust was something most foster kids struggled with, especially when they're placed in multiple homes. Fox was no different. He had tried to learn to trust but couldn't. He felt it was better that way.

"Fox?" Cyanide called.

"What?" Fox snarled.

"Your father is gone," Cyanide pointed out.

"We'll deal with him later. For now..."

Fox decided to go ahead with his plan and put Samantha out of her misery. He drove his claw into her back, and grasped her spinal cord. With a harsh yank, he ripped it out, her violent screams and howls echoing in the background before silence settled over them once more.

The whole warehouse and the surrounding area fell into an eerie silence. The creature let out a howl and disappeared into the night.

The creature made it back home and headed to the back yard, standing on the beach and staring out at the ocean for a moment. It returned to normal, and Fox stood there not wanting to go inside just yet. Fox settled into the hammock and rocked slowly, letting the breeze that had been coming off the water soothe his nerves.

He had just killed a person. He wasn't freaking out as most people would, but then again he wasn't most people. He didn't freak out when finding his dreams about being fused and becoming Cyanide were true. He wasn't sure why he didn't freak. Maybe he was jaded or maybe he felt this was better than the hand life had previously dealt him. Maybe he really died and this was Purgatory. He just didn't know.

"They were also trying to kill me, so it was self-defense. It's not like they can trace it back to me anyway. Apparently, the cult that my mother was once a part of is now mostly or completely extinct, and the ink? The only other thing I left behind besides blood is ink. Who the ever fuck can trace that back to me?" Fox asked himself.

"*What the hell are you mumbling about?*" Cyanide rumbled.

"Wouldn't you and the principal like to know?" Fox snarked.

"*Who is the principal person you speak of?*"

"No one. It's a figure of speech," Fox groaned.

"*If you say so. What do we do about your father?*" Cyanide asked with a growl.

"I say we let him come to us."

"*How do you know he will?*"

"Oh, he will. He still has a job to do and won't stop until it's done. It seems like Daddy Dearest has a one-track mind."

"*What'll we do until then?*"

"Not much we can do, but I don't think we'll have to wait for very long. With his partner now dead he'll want my head on a silver platter even more, and I bet it won't matter if they had a connection or not," Fox pointed out.

"*So we just sit here and wait?*" Cyanide asked, not liking that idea at all.

"Yup," Fox said, popping the P. "Although we could have a little fun while we wait."

"*What kind of fun?*" Cyanide asked wearily.

Fox smirked like the cat that caught the canary and watched the black veins crawl up his arm then disappear. He yawned and decided it could wait until tomorrow.

Episode 17

The next day, two teens were at the cliffside along one the shorelines of the island. Alex and Baxter were celebrating. They had successfully robbed a small grocery store and got away with it. They only wished their favorite punching bag was around to pin the blame on. They clinked their beer bottles and they each took a drink.

"That was amazing. What a rush. Those idiots didn't even know what was going on," Baxter said.

"So much for their security cams. You would think we would've been caught. It was way too easy," Alex said. "The cashier should've known better not to abandon her post and leave her till unprotected."

"Yeah. We got lucky this time. Next time, we should do it at night when everyone is gone. We could probably get away with more money," Baxter said, then took a sip of his beer.

"Dude, I'm telling you. We should rob a bank next," Alex said.

"Are you nuts?! We'd definitely get caught. I ain't going to prison."

"Come on, don't be a pussy. What are you afraid of? The supposed "Ink Murderer" that might not even be real?" Alex taunted. "Come on. The police probably cooked that one up."

"If he or she isn't real, then how did that girl on the news get her spine viciously yanked out?" Baxter asked.

"Man, I don't know, another crazy serial killer," Alex scoffed with an eye roll.

"Man, I don't know what to think. You know our island has a bad history with magic. Hell, maybe all of Hawaii has a bad history with magic. Damn...I should've paid better attention in school," Baxter said with a hint of fear and a shudder.

"Pfffft! It's all a bunch of hocus-pocus nonsense. Magic ain't real," Alex said.

"You don't know that! What about that freaky cult that used magic to commit all those crimes."

"Dude, would you stop? Magic. Ain't. Real!"

"Magic ain't real? Well, damn. That kills everything I believe in," a voice behind them growled.

Alex and Baxter stood, eager to beat the shit out of their favorite punching bag. The two boys looked around to spot him, but couldn't see anyone.

"Where are you kitty? Come on out. I promise not to hurt you," Alex said, making kissing noises.

"Yeah! Here kitty, kitty," Baxter taunted.

"Still as dumb as ever I see. How in the fresh hell did you two even graduate? No wait, let me guess! Mommy and Daddy bribed the principal? Lord knows you didn't get into college on your own," Fox questioned with his own taunts.

"Hey! We earned those scholarships!" Alex exclaimed.

"If that helps you sleep at night, but you and I both know that that's bullshit as well. Football will only get you so far and you suck at the game!"

"You little pussy! Get out here and take your beating!" Alex yelled.

"Fine. Fair warning, though, I'll be the one doing the beating," Fox said.

"Sure you will," Baxter scoffed.

"Don't say I didn't warn you," Fox said.

The two looked around until they spotted Fox lounging underneath a shady tree, humming to himself as he doodled. Fox looked up at the boys and smiled.

"Howdy fellas! Just let me clean up my mess here and I'll beat you in a moment," Fox said as he put away his things.

"Get up asshole! I'll teach you to degrade me!" Alex screamed, face red with rage.

Fox whistled and taunted, "Look at you pulling out big kid words."

Fox stood up and brushed himself off. He stepped out of the shadows, revealing his ashen skin and black veins. He looked dead to the other two boys, and they stumbled away from him.

"What the fuck?" Alex screamed.

"Stay back demon!" Baxter screamed and took a step back.

"Demon? That hurts. Really, guys," Fox said with a pout.

"*Am I not considered a demon?*" Cyanide questioned.

"Hmm. Good question, bud. I'll have to address that...right now. No. We are not. A monster, yes. A demon, no."

"*What's the difference?*" Cyanide asked.

"A demon is from Hell. Monsters not so much. Most of them are human," Fox explained.

"We're not monsters and who the fuck are you talking to!?" Alex demanded.

"To Cyanide. Allow me to introduce you," Fox said with a smirk that could shame the devil himself.

Fox used a trick he'd learned earlier that day to change faster. He allowed the ink pool around him and he quickly sunk into it. Just as quickly as he vanished, he reappeared as

Cyanide. The creature was on all fours but stood up on its hind legs looking down at the two humans.

Cyanide snarled and sneered at them as he noticed wet spots growing on their pants. Alex and Baxter were ghost white and trembled with fear. Cyanide stepped forward, and the two ran for their lives. Cyanide sat on the ground with a growl, hearing Fox roar with laughter.

"Satisfied?" Cyanide asked.

"*Very much so! Did you see them? They wet their pants!*" Fox laughed.

Cyanide shook his head.

"*Oh, come on. You know you enjoyed it,*" Fox said gleefully.

"All right. Yes, I enjoyed it a little. Why not kill them? As you said to Samantha they'll only come back to harm you," Cyanide asked curiously.

"*Nah. I think we scared them straight. They won't cause any more trouble.*"

"We should've been using this time to find your father," Cyanide growled.

"*He'll come to us. Be patient.*"

Cyanide went to say something when it was cut off by a loud BANG! The creature looked through the smoke and saw an explosive had gone off. It snarled. Maddox had to have been following them or known where they were going, and placed the device in between the trees to the left of them.

"*Dammit! He found us! I know that explosive was from him!*" Fox swore. Sure, he wanted his father to come to them but not like this.

"Was this a trap?" Cyanide asked with a growl.

"I don't think so. Alex and Baxter come here all the time. He must've followed us," Fox said. *"Either that or he somehow knew we were coming here and planted these devices."*

BANG! Another hidden explosive went off forcing Cyanide closer to the cliff.

"Shit! He's trying to force us over!" Fox exclaimed.

"So let's go over!" Cyanide barked.

"Problem! There's water at the bottom! Ink and water don't exactly go hand and hand, we need to switch back!" Fox shouted.

"You'll be hurt!" Cyanide snarled.

BANG! The creature is forced even closer to the edge. Fox took over and returned to normal with Cyanide growling at him. Another explosive went off, this time causing the edge of the cliff where Fox was standing to collapse entirely, sending him over.

Fox hit the water and swam to the surface. Once he broke through the water, he swam to shore and stumbled onto the beach. He looked up to a shadow dart away and heard the squeal of tires.

"Are you hurt?" Cyanide asked.

"A little shaken and maybe bruised in some places but overall, I'm fine," Fox gasped out in between coughs.

"What were you thinking?! You could've been hurt badly!"

"Ink and water don't mix. Look, we don't have time for a science lesson right now. We need to get up there and find that son-of-a-bitch. I have a feeling he knows we survived," Fox said after catching his breath.

"Do we go home first?" Cyanide asked.

"Yeah. I need to grab my bag, that and some dry boxers would be nice," Fox said shaking off out of instinct then shivered.

Fox climbed back up the cliff, grabbed his bag, and hopped in his car. He headed home, constantly looking in the rearview mirror to see if anyone was trailing behind him. So far, no one. Which was a good thing. Fox would hate to ruin his precious baby.

Episode 18

Fox arrived home and quickly changed into some dry clothes. He originally planned to shower but remembered he was on a mission.

"No point in showering right now. There's going to be a bloodbath," he muttered to himself.

"*Talking to yourself again? People will wonder if you're insane,*" Cyanide snarked.

"Nah. Talking to yourself is a sign of a healthy brain," Fox said as a matter-of-factly.

"*If you say so,*" Cyanide rumbled.

"I do say so. Now I say, it's go time! Well, not at this moment...later...but...you get it," Fox stammered.

Cyanide snorted and asked, "*Plan? Weapons?*"

"Improvise and avoid water. No weapons. I mean, we're no MacGyver but we don't need weapons," Fox said with a shrug.

"*Going in blind, again. Look how well that went last time,*" Cyanide growled.

"Hey, hey, hey. We took out one of the problems. Now it's time to take out the other. Stop your worrying, bud. We'll be just fine," Fox said nonchalantly.

Cyanide huffed a growl. The creature prayed its creator was right. While it had faith in him, the creature couldn't shake the feeling in its bones that something would happen. Whether it was good or bad, however, remained to be seen.

"*What now?*" Cyanide pondered.

"We leave at sunset and attack when it's dark. We'll use the ink to blend into the night," Fox said.

Cyanide made a noise of agreement and faded into the background to rest up. While Fox was all right, he was slightly injured from the fall and needed a little time to rest. He was tired from the incident earlier, the adrenaline it caused having worn off. Deciding a nap was in order; he climbed onto the bed and fell into a light but restful doze. He trusted Cyanide would wake him when the time came to get going.

Elsewhere-Unknown Location

Maddox was sitting in front of the workbench as he cleaned his guns and sharpened his blades. He probably didn't need to do all of this, but he wasn't going to risk anything. He remembered sneaking out of the warehouse and watching an unarmed Samantha get her spine violently yanked out of her back. He wasn't taking any chances. He even had traps set up in the forest behind him and on the lake beach in front of him.

Maddox placed the gun he was putting back together down and leaned back in his chair. He sighed and scrubbed a hand down his face.

'I really wish it hadn't come to this, son, but death is your only release from the poison that taints you now. It's for the best. It was for your mother. I know she's in Heaven free of it. You will be too. Very soon. I failed to protect you but I can still save you,' Maddox thought sadly.

Maddox picked the gun back up, put it together, and then loaded it. When that gun was assembled, he moved onto the next one. As he grabbed the next gun he saw the picture of his late girlfriend on the table with his tool kit. Maddox picked it up and looked at the girl in the photo, then sighed. He had kept it after all this time and carried it with him. He truly loved her once upon a time.

"I'll be sending Fox to you soon. You won't have to be alone up there anymore and you'll be free and happy. I'm only doing this because I loved you. Truly. I planned on asking you to marry me when the time was right. Fox was still a baby at the time. Then I found out who you really were and I had to save you. You ran from me and managed to hide until that night. I didn't want Fox to live the life he has, but I had no choice. You left me with no choice," Maddox said looking heavenward to his girlfriend.

Maddox took a deep breath. He was getting too worked up. He needed to be calm when his son came to try and kill him.

"Now I have no choice but to kill our only son and send him to you. I really don't want to...but orders are orders. It doesn't matter who you are or who your target is. When the boss gives you an order, you do it," Maddox said with a nod.

Maddox went back to cleaning his guns and loading them once they were done. Waiting was a pain in the ass. To him it was like being at the DMV. He just hoped he would show tonight.

Tonight was a good night to die.

Episode 19

Fox woke to Cyanide sharply barking in his ear. He groaned and rolled over. He cried out and fell out of bed when Cyanide roared in his ear.

Fox groaned then yawned groggily. "Damn, buddy. That was some wake-up call."

"*You were deeply asleep,*" Cyanide growled.

"Eck. That would explain the drool," Fox said, wiping his mouth.

Fox got up and stretched. He headed into the master bathroom, used the facilities, and then splashed cold water on his face to finish waking up. He went into the office and booted up the laptop to check something.

He smiled to himself.

"*What's got you so happy?*" Cyanide asked.

"My comic about you is a hit! People really like it!"

"*Is now really the time?*" Cyanide asked.

"Good a time as any. We have no clue how this is going to go down, so why not? Look. People are asking for more. This is amazing!"

"*We need to get going. Look outside,*" Cyanide rumbled.

Fox glanced outside and saw the sunset. "Hold on. Let me do something real quick."

Fox grabbed his comic pad and scanned the next pages in the story then quickly uploaded them. He decided to put them up for sale. It made him happy people were interested in Cyanide's story.

"All right. All good now. I'm ready to go."

"Are we taking your car or are we switching and running?" Cyanide asked, hopeful that they would run.

"Hell no! We are not taking my car! My baby will not be subjected to a bloodbath. We're switching and running. Besides, I have no idea where my father even is at this point, so we'll have to smell him out," Fox said.

Cyanide hummed in an answer. The creature had stated once before that the two had familiar blood so finding him shouldn't be too hard for him. He had given the creature the sense of smell despite the fact it's mostly a living skeleton, just in case its sight was ever cut off or it needed to find someone quickly. Its sense of smell was pretty amazing. Fox looked in the mirror and saw he was already ashen. He nodded to himself and headed downstairs and then outside to the beach. He allowed the ink to pool around his feet and then allowed Cyanide to take over.

"Are you ready?" Cyanide asked.

"As I'll ever be," Fox said with a hint of nervousness.

"Not having second thoughts, are you?"

"Not even in the slightest. Like I said once before, he'll keep coming back until we're six feet under. Completely and utterly dead. Hell, I bet he would try to separate us painfully first then kill us both. Although to kill you I have to die as well."

"Does he know that?"

"My mother's dead, isn't she?"

Cyanide said nothing in reply, but knew the boy was right. The creature his mother was tethered to died along with her that night. If Fox died, so would Cyanide. The creature would only be a comic book created by a lonely boy who once thought it was all just some dream he hoped to outgrow as he got older.

"Then let's avoid death. Shall we?" Cyanide asked with sarcasm.

"*You say that like it's easy,*" Fox snarked back.

"All right, enough. We need to get going. Yes, I can see in the dark and use my oversight to see heat signatures in pitch blackness, but I'd rather get there while there's still light."

"*Then let's go. You know what his blood smells like! His blood isn't mostly ink. So let's go!*"

Cyanide snorted but got to work. Once he had the scent he took off in the direction the smell was coming from. Cyanide reached the edge of the forest and was ready to go in to further search the area.

"*Wait! If my father is in these woods then we need to be really careful. There could be traps anywhere and everywhere,*" Fox warned.

"Got it," Cyanide said.

Cyanide entered carefully and kept a close eye out. The sun set as the creature ventured further and further into the woods. It jumped back when a metal jaw like thing jumped up and almost bit them.

"*Bear trap. Clever, Dad. Very clever. That thing would have snapped our leg off,*" Fox said.

"We need to get off the ground," Cyanide said.

"*The trees should hold us. We'll bounce from them until we get to my father,*" Fox said.

Cyanide nodded and jumped onto the thickest branch and hopped from tree to tree. Now they could avoid the traps. The creature made it to a shed by the dock on the lake. The shed was small and light shone from the small window.

"*He's there,*" Fox alerted.

"He is. Are you sure you're ready?" Cyanide asked.

"*I'm not backing out now,*" Fox said with determination.

"Good. We aren't leaving."

"*Switch back,*" Fox said.

"Why?" Cyanide demanded.

"*This fool and I need to have a chat first,*" Fox said.

"You can chat in this form. We need to be prepared," Cyanide reminded him.

"*Fine,*" Fox snapped.

The creature didn't revert back to human but the two switched minds. Fox was now Cyanide. It hopped down from the tree but stuck to the darkness the night provided. It looked at the tiny structure and howled.

Episode 20

At the dock shed, Maddox prepared himself for a fight which he didn't doubt Fox would put up. Maddox looked at his phone and saw it was now nine. He stood up and stretched. He half expected Fox to be here by now. Hell, he expected him hours ago.

"Wonder if he backed down. If he did, I'll have to go back to that house and get him," Maddox muttered to himself.

He jumped when a howl rang out, and looked out the window. It was too dark to see anything so he grabbed his phone and activated the flashlight app, shining it outside. He still couldn't see anything. He swore and went outside with a handgun drawn.

Maddox prayed it was only a normal wolf or even a coyote, then remembered there were none native to Hawaii. There weren't even foxes. He took in a deep breath to settle his nerves, but it did little to soothe his jumpiness. It was only his son for Heaven's sake.

"Fox? Is that you?" Maddox asked.

"Hello Maddox," Fox growled.

"Dad to you," Maddox said.

"No. You're no father of mine."

"I made you!" Maddox said.

"You're only the donor. Not a father. A father doesn't do what you did," Fox snarled.

"I had no choice! I had to save her and you! I failed in protecting her but I can still save you. Death is your only release. Plus, if I don't do it, someone worse will come and do it for me."

"Is that so? But which is it? Death is my only release or you have your orders?"

"It's both. I was ordered to kill your mother by the organization I work with. I didn't want to kill her, but it opened my eyes to the monster she was becoming, and I had to put her down before she poisoned or killed you. Samantha said it best though. Those in the syndicate can't have children. If they do, they are to be put to death along with the child. Your mother destroyed them one by one. She then continued on. That fortune she has, it's blood money. Son, please let me save you. Let me take you back to the mainland. My people can help you," Maddox pleaded. "I don't want to kill you."

"What a tragic tale. I give you points for the acting, though you need to work on it. It's really lacking." Fox yawned. "That and you're too conflicted. One minute you want to kill me, and the next you want to save me. Which is it?"

"Be serious," Maddox demanded.

"I am," Fox deadpanned.

"Fine. You got me. I was quite pleased to kill that bitch. I was going to kill you too that night, but sadly I was too injured. Your mother nearly killed me. After I recovered I was ordered to wait until you were older to kill you. They don't see children as threats. Then the order changed. My boss wanted to see if you would follow in your mother's footsteps. Here you are," Maddox growled.

"I make my own path," Fox said boldly.

"Last chance, son. Come with me or die."

Maddox heard laughing and then silence.

"How clichéd can you get? Come with me or die? That's the funniest shit I've heard. But I will give you that. After all, it's our first meeting in what...eleven years? Yeah. I'll cut you some slack, although it's not me who's going to die. Oh no," Fox/Cyanide said with a laugh.

It went silent again for a few moments and Maddox felt the cold, harsh wind on his back.

"You'll be the one to die," Fox/Cyanide whispered.

Maddox turned and fired his gun. He heard a thunking sound but knew he only hit a tree.

"Missed me! Missed me! Now you gotta kiss me! Wait...ewwwwww..." Fox taunted.

"Face me you coward!" Maddox snarled.

"What fun would that be?"

"Fox-" Maddox began.

"How can you even fight?" Fox/Cyanide asked. "It's pitch black out here. I have the advantage. Without the light, you can't even see in front of your face."

Maddox swore under his breath. The vile creature was right. Without the lantern glowing in the window, he couldn't see what was directly in front of him. Worse yet, he couldn't see that far as the lantern wasn't strong enough to illuminate much except the small shed he had been waiting in. He spotted his jeep and ran for it.

Fox inwardly swore and lunged for his father. He managed to knock his father away and watched as he rolled to a stop.

Maddox rolled over and fired a shot at the feet of the beast, watching it dance back away from the bullets.

Maddox darted into the woods with the beast tailing him. Maddox ran past a C-4 trap and activated it. The explosion sent Cyanide flying. He sprinted for the jeep and got in.

When it started he bolted, leaving his weapons and the creature behind.

"You want some fun? How about a little game of tag?" Maddox yelled back to Fox.

Luckily for Fox, Cyanide took over for a brief moment before the C-4 exploded and used the ink to protect them, but the creature was dazed. It came to an abrupt stop against a boulder. Cyanide heard the jeep turn on and then speed away.

"*Fox?! Are you all right?*" Cyanide asked concerned.

"I'm fine, bud. How about you?"

"*I am all right. Your father got away,*" Cyanide growled.

"Yeah, I noticed. I heard he wants to play tag? I'm game. Cyanide, you'll have to take over since you know what his blood smells like," Fox said.

Cyanide and Fox quickly switched, then took off into the woods. The creature used the trees like before, until it got to the edge of the forest. When its skeletal claws hit the ground it took off like Hell was on its tail. It stuck to the shadows as it tracked the man down.

Episode 21

"*How far out is he?*" Fox asked.

"Not much further! He's traveling at a rapid pace but nothing I cannot handle," Cyanide said.

"*We're getting close to the city, now. Remember we're on a small island with a small city, if people see us we're screwed.*"

"What would happen if we are caught?"

"*Mass hysteria and we'd wind up as lab rats. Remember in your one comic when you got caught by the government and taken to the mainland for testing?*" Fox asked.

"Yes, but I escaped. Surely it would not be that much of an issue?" Cyanide asked, not sure what the big deal was.

"*True, and yeah, it kinda would be, depending on where we would end up. Remember this: you were experimented on while you were there and it was painful to you. That same thing can happen to us if we're not careful,*" Fox reminded it.

"I see. Then we shall not get caught. The night is here and it shall be our ally."

When they hit the edge of the highway that led into the small city, Cyanide leapt on top of the buildings and ran across them, leaping from rooftop to rooftop.

"*There's the jeep!*" Fox exclaimed.

The creature spotted the jeep below and continued after it.

Maddox zipped off to the city, losing the creature for the time being. He looked up at the buildings above and somehow managed to spot the creature running after him.

"Sonovabitch!" Maddox swore.

Suddenly an ink-like spike was thrown right in front of him and he smashed into it. He was tossed from the vehicle and temporarily dazed. He got up and stumbled to the beach access, ignoring the people trying to help him.

Fox took this chance to leap off the roof, change back, and go down to his father.

"DAD!" Fox cried with false worry.

"*Fox, what are you doing?*" Cyanide growled.

Fox muttered to Cyanide, "Roll with me here." He then shouted again, "DAD!"

Fox weaved through the crowd and reached his father. He grasped his father's arm and gripped it tightly.

"Are you all right Dad? Do you need a hospital?" Fox asked, playing the worried son to perfection.

The crowd was getting bigger and closer. People were asking if they should call an ambulance.

"Do you know this boy, sir?" a woman asked.

"Yes. He's my son, and I'm fine, Fox. I don't need a hospital," Maddox said, playing along.

"Son, I would take your papa to the hospital, regardless," an elderly man said.

"That's the plan, sir. Come on, Dad, my car's this way," Fox said with a nod to the man.

Fox led him to a parking lot and then disappeared behind a car. After he made sure no one was watching, he steered the battered man to the beach and they walked a bit up the shore until they hit the private part of the beach. Fox was lucky there were no houses or condos, and the road was a way back on this portion. It was pitch dark, and the only sounds were the waves crashing on the sand.

"Get up. I know you're fine. You might be bruised but you're fine," Fox growled.

Maddox stopped playing his pitiful card and stood up.

"That was a good show, son. I didn't know you could form things from the ink," Maddox said with a bit of pride.

"I didn't, either. It was mostly Cyanide. I'm still learning everything." Fox crossed his arms over his chest.

"So how do we do this?" Maddox asked.

"Do you have to ask?" Fox asked with a wicked smirk.

POP POP POP!

Maddox tried to shoot the beast but he was blind as a bat in this darkness. The only light he had was the heat lightning and it was not bright enough to light up everything. He made do as he was still hung up on his mission.

Cyanide toyed with Maddox by knocking him over and then letting him up leaping off of him. The creature knew he could kill the man before him easily, hence the playing. The cycle repeated on for a few more moments until he ended up too close to the water.

Maddox fired the gun when the lightning lit up the sky once more and he saw the creature was forced to the water. He fired in that direction until he heard a splash and an unearthly screech of pain. Maddox smirked.

"What's the matter? Don't you like the water? You certainly love the beach," he taunted.

Fox didn't say anything, just snarled.

"Now that you've lost your skin what'll protect you?" Maddox asked wickedly.

"We haven't lost our skin," Cyanide reminded Fox. *"It can come back with the ink that flows in our veins. It'll take some time, however."*

"Shit! All right, so we kill him now and get it over with," Fox said.

Cyanide lunged for the man in the dark and pinned him to the ground. Maddox managed to kick the skeleton off. He fired his gun and got a few hits on the creature, breaking a few of the bones. Bullets cracked two ribs and its upper hind leg.

"You okay, buddy?" Fox asked concerned.

"I'm all right. Are you all right?" Cyanide asked.

"Fine. I can't even feel it. Are we really okay? I know in the comics this doesn't faze you," Fox said.

"We are fine. You're correct. These wounds do not faze us, as you say."

"Okay. I'm done playing games. We end this and end it now," Fox said with urgency.

"Are you done talking to yourself like a madman or do you need more time?" Maddox asked, getting a little impatient.

The creature snarled and gunned toward the man, knocking him flat on his ass once more. Cyanide then bit the man's arm and flung him to the water. Cyanide smirked in satisfaction when the man hit the water.

POP POP POP!

More shots were fired, but missed Cyanide completely.

Cyanide took Maddox by the leg and tossed him away again. It lunged at him, taking Maddox by his shoulder throwing the man up into the air then letting him crash back down to earth.

Maddox tried to get up, but his battered body wouldn't allow it. He looked over in the general direction of the creature and raised his gun.

CLICK. Maddox stared at his gun and tried to fire again. CLICK, CLICK. Nothing. Maddox threw the gun away in frustration.

"Looks like you're out of ammo, human. What a shame," Cyanide taunted with a growl.

Cyanide slinked closer to the broken man before him, ready to finish him off.

"Wait!" Maddox exclaimed.

Cyanide stopped and stared at the human.

"Please. Let me talk to my son again," Maddox said softly.

"*It's probably a trick! End it!*" Fox shouted.

"Why should I allow it?" Cyanide growled.

"Would you deny a dying man his last request?" Maddox asked.

"You are not dying. Not even close. Yes, you're badly injured, but not even close to death," Cyanide snarled.

"Just let me speak to my son. Please."

"It is up to you, Fox," Cyanide said.

"*Switch with me,*" Fox said, against his better judgment.

Cyanide allowed Fox to take over and Fox looked at the battered Maddox.

"What do you want?" Fox snarled.

"Fox, change back to you," Maddox said.

"Forgive me Pops, but I don't exactly trust you."

"Please just change back. My gun is empty, so I can't defend myself," Maddox said, raising his hands in a surrender pose.

Using what little ink had come back, he shifted back to mostly human. He still had some of Cyanide's features, such as the tail and his inky ears, his eyes were black with the pinprick white dots, his legs were still wolf-like, but the rest of him was human.

Fox walked up to his father with caution, stopping just a few feet short of him.

"Come closer son, I just want to talk," Maddox beckoned.

"Yeah, no. I'm fine right here," Fox said, making no moves.

"Suit yourself, I'll just come to you."

"One, if you can even get up. Two, stay back. I mean, I plan to kill you, don't get me wrong, but if you come anywhere near me I will drop you in a heartbeat," Fox threatened with a vicious snarl.

"I don't doubt it."

Maddox struggled to get up, and when he did, he was wobbly at first but held steady. He couldn't see his son, but looked where he thought he might be.

"I didn't want this, you know," he said.

"Oh fucking spare me," Fox growled.

"Despite what I've said, I meant it. I didn't want this and I wanted you to come with me," Maddox swore.

"The mind really is the first thing that goes, isn't it? You keep saying that, then you turn around and say the opposite. Which is it?" Fox asked.

"Fox-" Maddox began

"Let me tell you what I think. I think you fell in love with the one. You settled down but you barely knew each other. You both were leading double lives. She would disappear in the night as you would the day. Then I came along. The two of you found out what was really beneath the surface, and it scared you. She takes me and runs again, risking coming back here to raise her baby. You despise magic. You had to take her out on your boss's orders and your own. She died and you lived. You watch over me all these years, keeping tabs, and now you want to get rid of the nightmare once and for all. The kicker? I don't think you give a damn at all, hell you probably never gave a damn. You've been doing this for years and you let your group of merry men corrupt you. Make you think magic is evil. Newsflash asshole, the unknown and different aren't evil. Anyone that thinks that needs a good look in the mirror," Fox snarled.

Silence filled the beach.

Episode 22

The silence of the beach had been broken by Fox as he laughed.

"*Fox-*" Cyanide began.

"You got me doing a monologue like a B rated villain!" Fox laughed like a madman. "You dickless wonder, you."

Fox laughed for a few more moments before staring at his father, emotionless. Heat lightning lit the sky just enough for Maddox to see the hollow eye sockets and white pinprick dots staring into his soul. He visibly shuddered.

Fox noticed and smirked. Heat lightning revealed his face, showing Fox's fangs.

"Scared?" Fox asked.

"No," Maddox lied. He was terrified.

"You should've brought your brown pants," Fox growled.

"Your mother didn't scare me and neither do you," Maddox said.

"Liar liar, pants on fire," Fox sang.

Maddox began walking toward Cyanide, surprising it. Maddox heard Fox snarl a warning. Maddox and Fox looked up when it began to rain and lightning really lit up the night.

"Really!? Why is it always raining at the most dramatic part of the freaking movie!?" Fox shouted.

Fox snarled again and reverted to normal before the rain could take away the little ink he and Cyanide got back.

Maddox made his move and tackled Fox to the ground. The two rolled around until Fox kicked Maddox off of him. Fox flipped back up and took a fighting stance.

"*Fox, let me take back over,*" Cyanide said.

"I got this. Besides, it's raining. We can't risk it," Fox said.

Cyanide knew Fox was right, but still, he needed to help! Fox was getting exhausted.

"*Fox-*" Cyanide began.

"I got this, bud. I can take him," Fox said.

Just after saying that, Maddox came at him blindly swinging a knife. After being Cyanide a few times, Fox was now able to see in the dark.

"Smart move, you chocolate dipped screw head," he growled.

"The lightning helps. I hope it keeps storming," Maddox growled back.

"Fucking poetic rain. I hope it stops," Fox snarled with an eye roll.

He dodged a swing, the knife just barely missing his nose. Fox reached out and grabbed his father's wrist, then slammed a fist into the man's face.

Maddox stumbled but didn't go down until another fist slammed into his eye. Maddox managed to slash Fox on his calf. Fox yelped in pain and jumped back. Maddox got back up and began to beat Fox.

As he was being beaten, Fox was reminded of Mike and the other abusive homes he had lived in. With Cyanide barking at him and the flashes of abuse whizzing around in his head, he turned the tables and started beating Maddox, a man twice his size, to a bloody mass on the beach. He stopped when his father was unrecognizable.

"Suck it," Fox spat.

"*Are you okay, Fox?*" Cyanide asked, wishing Fox would switch with it.

"I'm good, bud. Gonna be sore tomorrow, but I'm good," Fox fibbed. He was hurting and exhausted.

"Let us finish our mission," Cyanide said.

"Yeah. Let's send the old man to his maker and go home," Fox agreed.

Before Fox could transform his arm just for a few moments, he felt a white-hot pain in his stomach. Fox howled and let Cyanide take over for a brief moment. A skeletal claw formed quickly and stabbed the man in the chest. This time the claw yanked out the heart and tossed it into the ocean. As fast as the claw came, it vanished. Fox panted like he had just run a marathon and the pain was right up there with the pain he experienced when he was shot.

"Fox! Let me take over, right now!" Cyanide exclaimed with urgency.

"What h-happened...to d-dealing more d-damage? We also got an ink p-p-problem right now..." Fox groaned.

"Forget that now! We're closer to the hospital this time and how would you explain this to the police!?" Cyanide barked with a snarl.

"Point t-taken...al-all right...g-go..." Fox panted out in pain.

Cyanide took over and transformed with Fox's screams of agony breaking the silence of the beach. When Cyanide was fully transformed he took off running along the darkened beach.

Cyanide felt Fox fading and it prompted him to run faster. When it got close enough to where the hospital was, the creature took to the rooftops. Cyanide was heading to the hospital that took care of Fox before.

Episode 23

Cyanide made it to the Beachfront Memorial Hospital and hopped across three rooftops and landed on the hospital roof. Cyanide stuck to the shadows so as to not freak out the patients as it climbed down to the ER entrance. It howled loudly to alert anyone in the ER. It quickly reverted back to Fox and the boy crawled slowly into the light before passing out.

A doctor came running out with a medical bag and a security guard and spotted the bleeding young man on the ground. The female doctor rushed up to him and gasped.

"Fox Kane? Oh god, what has happened to you this time?" Katrina gasped.

She jumped into action and began to stabilize the young man. She turned to the guard that came out with her. "Quick, get me a gurney and grab a nurse!"

"On it!"

The guard rushed inside and came back with a nurse and gurney. The nurse got right to work in helping the doctor to get the young man stable.

"Go inside and book an OR, stat. He needs surgery and fast." Katrina said.

"Right away doctor!" the nurse responded.

"Help me get him on the gurney." Katrina said to the guard.

He nodded and helped lift Fox onto the gurney and then wheeled him inside. The nurse the doctor sent in came rushing up to them.

"OR 5. Dr. Jensen is waiting to help," the young nurse said.

"Great, I'm going to need help," Katrina said.

The nurse and doctor rushed Fox to the OR where the other doctor was waiting. She scrubbed up as the young nurse and an older one with a medical assistant cleaned and prepped the bleeding Fox.

Fox was wheeled into the room and placed on the table. He now sported IVs, a blood bag, a ventilator, and was hooked to all the proper machines. Doctor Jensen entered the OR with Katrina surveying the patient.

"What do we have?" Jensen asked.

"A stab wound to the abdomen, multiple contusions, and a slash on his right calf." Katrina listed off. "In short, this boy was beaten and then stabbed."

"All right, people let's open him up and see the damage underneath." Jensen barked. "If a nurse could kindly stitch up his calf that would be fantastic."

A nurse volunteered and got to work leaving the doctors to do their jobs.

"What is this? His blood is black and thick." Jensen said curiously.

"Let's concentrate on saving the boy first and then you can play scientist," Katrina barked, needing him to focus on what's important right now.

"Right. Well, it seems the knife missed everything and anything vital, which is a good thing," Jensen said.

"Where's all this blood coming from then?" Katrina asked.

"Not sure."

"BP's dropping!" the anesthesiologist called.

"Shit!" Both doctors swore.

"Find out where that bleeding is coming from! Someone get another blood bag! Let's get this young man stable!" Katrina barked loudly.

The OR was in a fever pitch trying to save Fox. Machines continued to blare their warning until they stopped and the room stood still.

Episode 24

Fox moaned and moved his head back and forth to dislodge whatever was on his face. A gentle hand on his cheek stopped him.

"It's okay. You're all right now. Just rest," a voice said soothingly.

Fox drifted back off to dreamland where he joined Cyanide. He woke up later that day and looked around the room. It looked kinda familiar.

"Are you awake this time?" the same voice from before asked.

Fox flinched, not entirely awake yet.

"That sounds familiar," Fox mumbled sleepily.

"Glad you remember me," the voice said happily.

Fox blinked to clear his cloudy vision and looked over to his left where the voice was coming from. It was the same doctor that treated his gunshot wound and helped him.

"Dr. Katrina?" he rasped.

"Hey, you. Long time no see," she said with a smile.

She helped Fox take a few sips of water. He cleared his throat and spoke again.

"How long have I been out?"

"About four and a half days. You're banged up pretty bad. Not to mention the exhaustion," Katrina said. "Better than two weeks."

Fox nodded. "I'll give you that one. I'll take four days rather than two weeks."

"Uh-huh," she hummed.

Fox shifted nervously, and stopped when pain flared up in his side. He squeezed his eyes shut.

"Easy. I'd hate to have to cut you open again," Katrina scolded.

Fox nodded and took a few deep breaths. He looked over at the doctor with a smile. Fox made himself as comfortable as he could and relaxed.

"I was hoping not to see you again. No offense," he joked.

"I was hoping for the same thing. So none taken," she joked back.

"What's with that face?" Fox asked, noticing her body language was off.

Katrina raised an eyebrow and looked at Fox like she didn't have any look on her face.

"Not sure what you mean," she fibbed.

"You know, don't you?"

"That your blood is black? Yeah, I know. Fox, what happened to you?"

Fox carefully explained what had happened, from the spells up until this point. Katrina blinked. She couldn't believe what she just heard, but somehow knew Fox wasn't lying.

"Fucking magic," she swore.

"You don't believe me, do you?" Fox asked.

"No, I believe you. Hawaii has a history with magic, but not all of it bad. I'm just upset you were dumb enough to try something like that and it actually worked," Katrina explained.

"If it makes you feel better, I didn't expect it to work either," Fox said sheepishly.

Katrina nodded and asked, "So, now what?"

"What do you mean?"

"I mean what do you plan to do with this?"

"If you're talking about becoming some type of superhero, I hate to burst your bubble but I'm no hero," Fox said with loving snark.

"Did I say superhero? Although it couldn't hurt. Hawaii could use a hero to look up to. New York has too many as it is," Katrina smiled.

"Let the little guys have some fun now, right?" Fox asked with a chuckle.

"Exactly."

"I still don't think I'd be a hero. Heroes aren't scary," Fox yawned and then frowned as a thought hit him. "Whoa, whoa, whoa! Why are you suddenly helping me? Shouldn't you and the government be dissecting me by now?"

"Do you want to be a lab rat?" Katrina raised an eyebrow.

"No..." Fox said looking down.

"Okay then. I'm helping you, besides you need someone to look after you," Katrina said with a motherly tone.

Fox opened his mouth to argue when the doctor raised her hand to silence him.

"I've been keeping the others from turning you into a lab rat and such. When my partner found any blood we gave to you turned to ink, he wanted to experiment right then and there."

"Thanks for sparing me," Fox said.

"You're welcome. We'll talk later, you still need rest," Katrina gently patted his leg.

Fox nodded and let the good doctor check him over before drifting back off to sleep. Fox woke up late the next night and sat up. He started to remove all the tubes and wires he was hooked up to.

"Hey, bud?" he asked.

"*Fox. Are you well enough to escape?*" Cyanide rumbled.

"I'll be all right. We need to get out of here, though. If one doctor knows about my inky blood, the whole hospital probably knows. Hell, the doc said herself she's had to keep others away from taking us to any labs already. I'm surprised she's left us alone knowing the other doctors want to cut us open and see what makes us tick."

Fox made his way around the room and found some sweats and a t-shirt someone left behind. He got dressed and put on slippers.

"*I heard the doctor whilst you slept. She locked us in and the others need her key,*" Cyanide rumbled with a slight growl.

"One, what the hell kind of hospital has doors where the doctor can lock their patients in? Two, that makes me feel better, but we still need to go."

"*Agreed. No transformation. Your body needs a lot of healing from the damage not only from your father but from when you let me take over to bring you here,*" Cyanide said, not happy.

"Great. So what then?" Fox huffed tiredly.

"*We do the same thing we did the last time.*"

"I blend in with the shadows. Sounds like a plan." Fox gave a thumbs up.

Fox allowed the ink to flow and turn him into a shadow. He walked up to the door and ink pooled to the floor. Fox sunk into the puddle but didn't transform, just slid under the door and rose up from the ink on the other side.

"The ink never ceases to amaze me. I wonder what else I can do," Fox said in delight.

"*Wonder later, we must go,*" Cyanide urged.

"Right." Fox stuck to the shadows and began his journey home.

Katrina came back to check on Fox with a backpack in one hand and a blanket and pillow in the other. She unlocked the door and stepped inside.

Fox was nowhere to be seen.

"Damn that boy," Katrina swore. She turned and left.

Episode 25

A few months later-West Point Beach.

A man stumbled as he tried to run from the thing that had been chasing him. This man had come to the small island from the mainland after committing a string of murders, to hide from the police chasing him.

Now there was something worse chasing him. A living breathing nightmare.

"Get away! Leave me alone!" the man screamed in fear.

"Run, run as fast as you can! You can't outrun me, I'm a new kind of Cyanide!" the growling voice taunted.

The man sprinted faster and didn't notice a branch on the ground, he tripped. He tried to get back up but his legs felt like jelly. He looked to see the silhouette of the thing chasing him.

"Get back! Stay away from me you monster!" the man screamed.

"Monster? That stings. Every time someone calls me that, it still smarts. It's been months!" the voice said with mock hurt. "I'm just messing with you!"

"You're crazy!" the man shouted.

"That's better!" the voice said cheerfully.

A smell wafted in the air as the man whimpered in fear. He flinched when he heard the beast laughing.

"Just like my bullies. They had weak bladders as well. You should really consider wearing or at least carrying diapers," the voice mocked with a laugh.

"*Fox, stop toying with him and just end it*," Cyanide said, coming through.

"Aw, you're no fun bud!" Fox whined.

"*Fox-*" Cyanide warned.

"All right, all right. Bossy much," he said with a pout.

The creature stepped into the light one of the street lamps provided. The man screamed in horror and tried to scramble away, but failed miserably. His screams turned to howls as the beast lunged at him viciously ripped out the heart.

Fox tossed the heart next to the head and ran off into the night.

Cyanide walked down the private beach until it came to its home. Fox reverted back to normal and stretched. He hopped into the hammock and rocked, gazing at the moon while listening to the waves crashing on the shore.

"That was fun!" he said cheerfully. "The news was wrong, though. There's no way he was a serial killer if he was scared of moi, but hey, one less murderer in the world. Dexter Morgan eat your heart out."

"*You need to shut up during our hunts,*" Cyanide growled.

"Ugh," Fox groaned with an eye roll.

"*Honestly, the whole "Run run as fast as you can" bit? What was that?*"

"Catchphrase! All the greats have one," Fox explained happily.

"*It's stupid.*"

"Is not!" Fox argued.

Cyanide huffed a growl.

"The night's still young. Fancy another hunt?" Fox itched to get back out there.

"Not after tonight's hunt," Cyanide deadpanned.

"Oh, come on!" Fox pleaded. "I'm sure the police scanner is picking up on something."

"I said no. Now shut up and rest," Cyanide growled like an irritated parent.

Fox pouted, but listened to the wolf-like creature. He closed his eyes and let the swaying hammock rest him. He reopened his eyes on a thought, well more like a feeling that's been bothering him for a while.

"You know, hunting bad guys is fun and all but I got this feeling we've got a bigger problem heading our way."

"Oh?" Cyanide hummed.

"Yeah. I mean it's only a feeling at the back of my mind, but you never know," Fox shrugged

"If there is, we will be fine," Cyanide rumbled softly.

"You're right. It's all good. We're all good," Fox said.

A comfortable silence filled the air once more, but didn't last. Fox sat up quickly up then rushed into the house.

"Fox? What is it? What's the matter?" Cyanide asked, on alert and ready for danger.

"I'm so stupid! I can't believe I fucking forgot!" he reprimanded himself.

Fox ran up the stairs to his new office/art studio and rushed to his desk. He woke up his laptop and brought up the latest comic pages, then uploaded them.

"A little late, but hey, my readers will be happy to wake up to new pages."

"You're a bleeding idiot!" Cyanide snarled.

"Oh, come on, bud! Don't be mad!"

"*I thought something was wrong the way you rushed about!*" Cyanide growled.

"Well yeah. I forgot to upload." Fox argued.

Cyanide growled again and ignored Fox.

"Cyanide? Please don't be mad! Hey, at least I make good money off these comics. I'm the next Stan Lee!" Fox proclaimed loudly and proudly.

Cyanide huffed a growl as Fox continued to ramble on being famous and the greatest.

"I'm going to be a legend!"

"*In your own mind maybe,*" Cyanide snarked.

Fox's jaw dropped.

"Oh, you are so gonna get it, bud!" Fox shouted.

"*Bring it, string bean,*" Cyanide mocked.

The two bantered back and forth until Cyanide decided to take over and forced the boy to sleep and rest. Fox protested at first but fell to sleep eventually, making Cyanide smirk in triumph.

Cyanide then pondered on what Fox had said earlier. It felt something was off too, though it wasn't sure what. Whatever it was, Cyanide would make sure Fox was ready to tackle it with it by his side.

Bonus scene

In an unknown location, the room was dimmed with only candles as the source of illumination. A hooded figure walked along the rows of candles. The figure kneeled before a throne.

"Mistress," she greeted.

"My child," the woman on the throne said.

"Lady Katrina Alaverez has arrived," the hooded woman relayed.

"Thank you, my child. You are dismissed," the woman on the throne said with a wave.

The girl stood and bowed. She turned and left as Katrina entered the room wearing the same outfit as the girl: the traditional outfit was a silk black skirt with a slit on both sides revealing both legs up to the hip, the top was a black sports-bra like garment showing off the stomach, with a large hooded cloak to finish the look. Katrina kneeled as the girl did before.

"Mistress Doris."

"Katrina. It's wonderful to have you back," Doris said with a smile.

"It is an honor, my Mistress. I've missed my home," Katrina returned the smile.

"As we have missed you," Doris said. "You may stand."

Katrina stood.

"Is it definite, then? Fox is the creature?" Doris asked hopefully.

"Yes, Mistress," Katrina confirmed.

"We must prepare then. The son will return home, at last. Keep your eye on him, Katrina," Doris commanded.

"Yes, Mistress."

The candles blew out, plunging the room into darkness.

Don't miss out!

Visit the website below and you can sign up to receive emails whenever Emily Hagenbaugh publishes a new book. There's no charge and no obligation.

https://books2read.com/r/B-A-LOYQ-QGGVB

BOOKS 2 READ

Connecting independent readers to independent writers.

www.ingramcontent.com/pod-product-compliance
Lightning Source LLC
LaVergne TN
LVHW010536200726
843506LV00013B/2837